BEACHFRONT BAKERY:

A KILLER CUPCAKE

(A Beachfront Bakery Cozy Mystery —Book One)

FIONA GRACE

Fiona Grace

Debut author Fiona Grace is author of the LACEY DOYLE COZY MYSTERY series, comprising nine books (and counting); of the TUSCAN VINEYARD COZY MYSTERY series, comprising five books (and counting); of the DUBIOUS WITCH COZY MYSTERY series, comprising three books (and counting); and of the BEACHFRONT BAKERY COZY MYSTERY series, comprising six books (and counting).

Fiona would love to hear from you, so please visit www.fionagraceauthor.com to receive free ebooks, hear the latest news, and stay in touch.

CHAPTER ONE

"Where are those crème brûlées, Allison?" Russell barked, from the opposite end of the busy kitchen. "Table five's still waiting!"

Ali Sweet narrowed her eyes at her boss. She hated the way he yelled at her like a kid. But there wasn't much she could do about it. Landing a coveted job at one of the finest French restaurants in Los Angeles made her a very, very lucky woman. Not that Ali felt particularly lucky…

She'd joined three years ago as a pâtissier. It was supposed to be her dream job. She'd trained years for it. But thanks to her mean boss, her dream job had quickly turned into a nightmare.

"Don't just stand there!" Russell yelled, snapping his fingers. "Chop chop!"

With a reluctant sigh, Ali made her way across the hot, noisy, crowded kitchen of Éclairs to the ovens. She pushed her thick, dark blonde braid over her shoulder and peered in through the oven window to assess the fiftieth batch of crème brûlées she'd made that day. By now, she'd made more crème brûlées than there were traffic jams in LA.

"They just need a couple more minutes," she called over her shoulder to Russell.

Though Russell's beady brown eyes stayed fixed on his chopping, Ali noticed his nostrils flare with fury. *A couple more minutes* was clearly *not* the answer he'd wanted, and now he was going to blow.

Ali knew she was about to be on the receiving end of one of his epic meltdowns. She gulped with dread. But there was

muttered as he shook his head of dark hair. "A couple more minutes…" Then he stabbed his nowhere to run. She felt helpless.

"A couple more minutes…" Russell knife into the chopping board, swirled to face her, and yelled: "You have one task, Allison! One task! And you can't even do it right!"

His insult hit her like a slap across the face. Ali shrank back. She hadn't been a wallflower before the job, but thanks to Russell she felt beaten down.

1

None of the other chefs in the busy kitchen reacted to Russell's demeaning outburst, but Ali knew they were all watching her out of the corners of their eyes. She could feel their side glances burn into her like lasers. There was no such thing as an ally when it came to the kitchen of Éclairs.

"Sh—shall I serve them now?" Ali asked, her voice trembling. "They'll be a little underdone."

She already knew the answer was *no*, but Russell had put her in an impossible position between speed and perfection, and she had to say something.

"Of course I don't want you to serve them now!" Russell screeched. "This crème brûlée is for a Hollywood executive! It has to be perfect!"

Ali couldn't care less who the crème brûlée was for. It could be for the Pope and it would make no difference to her. She'd just about reached the end of her tether.

Suddenly, the sound of a loud metallic bang made Ali jump out of her skin. Russell had hit one of the hanging pots with a metal soup ladle.

"Don't just stand there!" he yelled. "Start on the next batch."

Ali scurried back to her workstation and began on the next batch of crème brûlées. She went through each step robotically—slicing the vanilla pod, scraping its seeds into the cream, whisking the egg yolk and sugar, setting the porcelain ramekins in their baths of water—all the while wondering wistfully where it had gone wrong.

She'd been thrilled, initially, to get a job at the exclusive Éclairs restaurant in Silver Lake, Los Angeles. Since her first class bachelor's degree in the Culinary Arts hadn't been sufficient for the high-end restaurants, she'd headed back to school and completed a further postgraduate advanced degree in Culinary Innovation. *Still* unable to get the job she was after, she'd then studied for her doctoral degree while completing an apprenticeship under the tutelage of master chef Milo Baptiste.

Milo had been an inspiring tutor. His passion for cuisine was infectious. His knowledge of food was vast. Under his direction, Ali had felt like she was destined for greatness, the Ernst Pauer to his Wolfgang Mozart. Thanks to Milo, she'd found her culinary flair.

At first it seemed her efforts had paid off. She quickly secured an interview at Éclairs, which was basically the Vienna State Opera House of restaurants. But then Russell had assigned her to crème brûlée duties. Crème brûlée and nothing more.

Reality hit. Instead of performing to adoring crowds, Ali was playing the same uninspiring pop hit over and over again. This was not how her career was supposed to turn out and Ali was just about ready to lose her mind from the monotony of it all.

The bleep of the oven alarm brought Ali out of her ruminations. The batch was finished.

She went to the oven and removed the crème brûlées, set them on the counter, and lit her blowtorch. If someone had told her back in culinary school that one day she'd be bored with burning food with fire, she would've laughed them out of the kitchen. And yet, here she was, wielding a blowtorch, turning the top layer of sugar on the crème brûlées to a bubbling golden brown, feeling nothing.

She finished each brûlée off with a perfectly placed sprig of spearmint, then delivered the batch to Russell, forcing her blank face into a wan smile.

"I present to you, the perfect crème brûlée," she announced.

Russell peered down his bony nose at each individual ramekin, inspecting them thoroughly. He offered no praise at all. He simply plucked out the one he wanted delivered to Mr. Hollywood at table five, and dinged the brass bell for a server. Ali wasn't surprised. She'd long ago given up expecting praise from her boss.

A swarm of attractive young servers appeared at the serving hatch. They were all aspiring actors, desperate to be the one to deliver the crème brûlée to a Hollywood exec. But Ali had no interest in the fate of her dessert. She was midway through the next batch, after all, so she slunk back to her position, shoulders slumped, burdened by the weight of her unspent talent.

She rolled her eyes up to the ceiling tiles—tiles she'd stared at so many times she knew every grease spot and projectile tomato juice stain.

Please let something change, she thought.

Just then, a voice called from the serving hatch: "Table five wants a word with the chef."

Surprised, Ali swirled on the spot to look at the hatch. Troy, the handsome young server with the flawless dark skin and inviting smile, was eagerly drumming his fingers on top of it, his dark eyes on her.

"Did he say why?" Ali called back, acutely aware that every pair of eyes in the kitchen was now fixed on her.

Troy shook his head. "He just asked me to bring you out."

3

Ali swallowed anxiously and hurried across the kitchen, self-consciously pushing stray strands of blond hair out of her face as she caught snippets of whispers from the other chefs. Before she left through the swinging doors, she smoothed down her apron. Then she headed through them and paused beside Troy.

"Did he look mad?" she whispered, craning her head closer.

"Hard to tell," Troy replied in an equally discreet murmur.

It's fifty-fifty then, Ali thought apprehensively. Either Mr. Hollywood was so impressed by her crème brûlées he was about to buy the rights to her life story and turn it into the next feel-good indie blockbuster, or he was so dissatisfied he felt the need to tell her to her face. Of course, the former wasn't likely, but Ali knew the latter wasn't either. Her crème brûlées were perfect. Milo Baptiste had told her so himself. In fact, his exact response had been, "Someone needs to invent a new letter to come before A in the alphabet, because these are better than A star!" followed by an outpouring of European-style cheek kissing.

She tried to muster that confidence as she began the long walk across the marble floor to table five, cautiously weaving through the elegant sandalwood dining tables so as not to interrupt any of the diners enjoying their expensive evening out at the classy establishment.

She reached table five. Each of the red velvet chairs surrounding the round table was filled with an overweight white man in a black dinner suit. The men were distinguishable only by their varying degrees of baldness.

Ali nervously clasped her hands together. "Did someone ask to speak to me?"

The man who'd overcompensated for his receding hairline by growing a goatee looked her up and down with piercing, pale gray eyes. Ali's crème brûlée sat untouched in front of him.

So this is Mr. Hollywood, Ali thought.

"I did," he said.

Ali felt scrutinized under his gray-eyed stare. She tugged the collar of her chef's coat, feeling suddenly restricted by it.

"What can I do for you?" she asked, forcing herself to sound genial.

The man slowly pulled the spearmint sprig from his untouched crème brûlée and held it up to the light.

"Anything look amiss?" he asked.

Ali peered at the sprig. She saw no eyelash attached to it. No dead fruit fly stuck to its leaves. It was a normal sprig of perfectly nice spearmint. Better than normal, really, since it came from a local organic produce store.

"It looks fine to me," Ali said.

"IT HAS THREE LEAVES!" the man suddenly yelled.

Ali jumped. Her eyes pinged all the way open with surprise. Every single patron in Éclairs froze and turned to look. An uncomfortable silence descended on the restaurant.

"I'm sorry?" she asked, bewildered.

"COUNT THEM!" the man bellowed. He pointed at each leaf in turn. "ONE. TWO. THREE!"

His face was turning quite red. By the sensation of heat creeping into her cheeks, Ali assumed hers was too.

"I don't understand," she said, finally.

Mr. Hollywood threw his napkin onto the table and rose to his feet.

"Spearmint should have four leaves," he said, stepping close until his face was just an inch from hers. "FOUR!"

His yell was so forceful, spittle flew into Ali's face.

Ali blinked—appalled, disgusted, and totally dumbfounded. She'd dealt with angry customers before, but nothing like this.

She glanced back toward the hatch appealingly. Troy was still standing where she'd left him, watching on helplessly. There was nothing he could do to help. In the strict hierarchy of Éclairs, the servers were even lower than the chefs. The only person who could rescue Ali from the situation was Russell.

Just then, she spotted her boss through the hatch. He was watching the whole thing with a satisfied smirk on his face.

Ali realized, with burning humiliation, that Russell had no intention of helping her. In fact, he appeared to be relishing her misery.

Suddenly, a surge of calm clarity overcame Ali. She looked over at table four, where one of the crème brûlées from the same batch had been delivered, and plucked the spearmint from it. The woman who'd been eating it let out a horrified gasp.

"Excuse me, I just need to borrow this," Ali said, calmly.

She turned back to Mr. Hollywood and held the sprig out to him between her pincered fingers. "One, two, three, four," she said, counting each leaf.

Then she slammed it into his uneaten crème brûlée.

The crispy sugar layer cracked, sending the gooey cream beneath exploding into the air. Cream splattered over every single bald head at the table.

5

The men leapt out of their seats so quickly their chairs tipped back and hit the marble tiles, sending loud thuds around the restaurant. Every single patron turned and began murmuring as the black-suited men started screaming angrily at Ali.

"Enjoy your meal," she said, serenely, as she untied her apron strings.

She threw her apron down on top of the mess she'd created, turned away from their angry red faces, and marched for the exit, her head held high as she ignored the stunned diners and open-mouthed servers she passed.

Just as she reached the door, she heard Russell's voice yelling from the kitchen across the entire restaurant.

"That's it, Allison Sweet! You're fired!"

Ali paused, her hand on the exit bar. A small, triumphant smile inched across her lips.

"Good," she said.

Then, feeling giddy with relief, she pushed the door open and exited into the hot LA sunshine.

She felt like she'd been released from prison. She was free! And she couldn't wait to get home to tell her boyfriend all about her triumphant victory over her bully of a boss.

CHAPTER TWO

"You did *what?*" Otis exclaimed.

He stared up from the couch at Ali standing in the doorway of their living room. His pale green eyes registered shock and disbelief.

"I quit," she repeated, adding more triumph to her tone. "Well, technically I was fired before I could quit, but the outcome is the same."

Otis ran his hands through his short Afro. He was wearing black sweatpants, the ones Ali joked were his uniform since he wore them as often as she did her apron. An apron she'd never have to wear again, she realized with borderline hysterical glee.

"Ali..." Otis said. "Please tell me this is a prank."

"Nope," she said jovially. She flapped a hand to get him to move over. "Scoot."

But Otis didn't move an inch. He was sitting completely still, frozen like a statue. "Are you honestly telling me you just quit your job?"

"Yes," Ali said, getting a little exasperated.

She'd been expecting more of a celebratory shock from him. Instead, his handsome features had become drawn. His milky brown skin had gone somewhat gray. Maybe it would just take a little while to sink in.

She wriggled her backside into the gap that Otis had failed to make bigger for her, and readjusted her thick golden braid over her shoulder. Feeling carefree, she stretched her legs out in front of her onto the coffee table, languorously crossing one over the other, and took a swig of beer from the open bottle on the table.

"I'm finally free," she sighed with a contented breath of fruity hops.

Otis flopped back against the couch and chucked his gaming controller into his lap. He tipped his head back and turned his gaze to the ceiling.

"Ali!" he moaned.

Ali was perplexed by his reaction. "What? You always complain we never get to spend much time together because Russell works me

7

like a dog. Well, now we can. Speaking of dogs, we should get one! I'll have the time to walk it now and—"

"Ali!" Otis exclaimed, turning to face her.

"What?" Ali cried, exasperated. "Why do you keep saying my name like that?"

Her boyfriend drew in a long, slow breath, as if ready to launch an attack. "Have you lost your mind? How are you going to pay for everything? The rent? The gas bill? The electricity?" He pointed to the lightbulb as a visual aid.

Ali felt her defenses go up. This was so not the congratulatory celebration she was expecting. She thought Otis would be happy for her for finally quitting the job that had made her miserable for so many years, but instead he was huffing and puffing away like a frustrated toddler.

"Well, why don't you get a job?" she countered. "You haven't been able to keep a full-time job since I've known you."

He narrowed his eyes. "That's not fair. You know it's impossible to work full time while auditioning."

Otis had been chasing his dream of becoming an actor for three years now, a pursuit Ali had pretty much been financing.

"You only care about electricity because of that thing," she countered, pointing to the paused computer game on the television screen—the object of most of the couple's arguments. "We could have a broken air conditioning unit and you wouldn't even notice the sweat as long as your game was working."

"You're changing the subject," Otis said, thinly.

Ali huffed. "Fine. To answer your questions. One: have I lost my mind? Nope. I've saved it. Because I was one crème brûlée away from a nervous breakdown. And we're talking Hannah Sweet–level breakdown."

The eldest of the Sweet siblings had taken the whole corporate path in life, and seemed to think periodic breakdowns were just part of the job.

Ali continued. "Two: how am I going to pay for everything?" She tapped her chin. "That's a good one. How am *I* going to pay for *everything*?" she repeated, with extra emphasis on the key words. "How about this? I won't! My days of paying for *everything* are done." She pinched one of his milky brown cheeks. "It's about time you pulled your weight around here."

Otis brushed her hand away, his brow deeply furrowed. "We had a deal. One year for me to see if I could land an acting job."

"I remember," Ali said. "And it's been exactly..." She gazed at an imaginary watch on her wrist. "...three years! Well, what do you know? The cash cow's run dry."

She dropped the jokiness and looked him dead in the eye. Otis looked distinctly unimpressed. He was an exceptionally handsome man but Ali found this expression of frowning distaste quite unattractive.

"I just landed a role," he stated, without emotion.

His statement knocked Ali off guard. Her big blue eyes widened. She was stunned into silence. She put the beer bottle down carefully on the coffee table, feeling her hands shaking a little as she did.

"You—you—" She couldn't get the words out. "Really? Otis? You got a role?" The excitement started rising in her chest, making her voice higher and higher pitched. "Congratulations!"

She threw her arms around him. It was what they'd been working toward for all these years. What they'd been hoping for. All the sacrifices she'd made had finally paid off. And what perfect timing. She wouldn't have to stress even half as much about her temporary unemployment now that Otis had found work.

But beneath her embrace, Otis was stiff.

Puzzled, Ali drew back and regarded him with querying eyes. "What's the matter?"

Otis rubbed his forehead, looking uncomfortable, not meeting her eyes.

"Otis?" Ali pressed. "Why aren't you celebrating? What am I missing?"

"It's a TV show," he said, sounding far from thrilled. "A sitcom."

"And that's... bad?" Ali guessed, feeling more confused by the second. "I thought you wanted a sitcom. You always said landing a sitcom was gold. The most regular paycheck in the business. I mean now really isn't the time to be picky."

"It's not in LA," Otis said simply.

"Okay..." Ali said, still not getting it. "Where is it?"

"New York," Otis told her. "For six months."

Was that the reason for his hesitancy? Because the job would be on the East Coast for half a year? Well, he needn't worry. With video calls and cheap domestic flights, going long distance for a few months was hardly a catastrophe.

"Those six months will fly by," Ali said, flapping her hand dismissively. "Come on. Let's get out the celebratory champagne."

They'd bought the bottle the first day they'd moved into their LA apartment, and it had sat at the back of the fridge for three years, waiting for Otis to get his big break.

She went to stand, but Otis stopped her with a hand on her arm.

"I don't want to do long distance," he said in a small voice.

Ali felt her eyebrows pull together. She sank back down into place. "You don't?"

Otis flashed her a pained expression. "No. I don't."

Ali mulled it over. If Otis didn't like the idea of long distance, that meant she'd have to leave LA and move to New York City. It wasn't something Ali had considered before, but Hannah was in New York, and it would give her time to spend with her niece and nephew. Besides, they'd only ever moved here to be close to Hollywood for Otis. There was no real reason for her to be in LA now she'd quit her job.

She turned to Otis and smiled kindly.

"I'll move with you," she said.

"Ali..."

She shook her head. "It's okay, Otis. I promise you I don't mind. Clearly the universe is sending us some kind of sign. Me losing my job the same day you land a role. Lady Fate must want us to be in New York now."

Ali wasn't usually one for "signs"—that was far more her brother Theodore's kind of thing—but she had to admit it felt like more than a coincidence.

She started picturing it; the skyline, the snowy winter, the *bagels*!

"It'll be an adventure," she said, dreamily. "Romantic."

"Ali..." Otis said again. "We're not moving to New York together."

Ali paused, even more confused than ever. "What? Why?"

The pained expression on Otis's face was even more pronounced than before, and Ali felt an ominous sensation descend upon her. Her heart began to race.

"What's going on?" she asked. "I'm obviously not getting something."

Otis drew in a long, deep breath. "I'm breaking up with you," he announced through his exhalation.

Ali was stunned into complete silence. She blinked. "Y—you're—"

"Breaking up with you," Otis repeated.

Ali's mouth went completely dry. Her mind swirled. This wasn't real. This wasn't happening.

"Why?" she squeaked. "I can come to New York. I honestly don't mind."

"It's not that," Otis said.

"Then what?"

He rubbed his face. "The show is... it's a gay sitcom. It's a gay sitcom, for gay men, on a gay TV channel run by a gay crew and acted by..." He sighed. "...a gay cast."

Ali narrowed her eyes as her brain tried to calibrate. "So... you're breaking up with me because you need to pretend you're gay?"

"No!" Otis cried, throwing his arms in the air with frustration. "I'm saying I have to break up with you because ... because ..." He took her by the shoulders and stared at her, pain in his pale green eyes. "Because I'm gay, Ali."

Ali felt all the blood drain from her face. She was too shocked to speak.

Otis continued. "At least, I'm like ninety percent sure I am. Things have been weird between us for ages..."

"They have?" Ali squeaked, her voice little more than a stunned whisper.

"You're never here," Otis continued. "We haven't slept together for months. I spend all my time with Colton." He was listing his one gay friend as if it proved some kind of point.

"And?" Ali challenged.

"And I mean I spend *all* my time with him," he said. "With him. Specifically."

It slowly dawned on Ali what Otis was implying, but her mind just couldn't comprehend.

"Are you telling me you're *sleeping* with Colton?" she demanded.

Otis took a deep breath, neither confirming nor denying her accusation. But he didn't need to. His silence spoke volumes.

"Is *Colton* going to New York with you?" Ali asked. The pitch in her voice was getting higher and higher, making her sound like a very angry Minnie Mouse.

"I don't know. Maybe. I don't know what I want. My head's all over the place."

"*Your* head's all over the place?!" Ali cried, leaping up from the couch. "Yours? I've just found out my boyfriend who I LIVE with in a

11

house I PAY for has been using me for three years so he can chase some silly dream of becoming an actor!"

Otis closed his eyes. "I knew you'd take this badly."

"Oh, did you?" Ali cried, incredulous. "Did you really? You must be a magician! A soothsayer! How clever of you to predict that when you told me you were cheating on me I'd take it badly!"

Minnie Mouse was gone. In her place was the Incredible Hulk. Ali was just about ready to rip off her shirt and punch a wall.

Otis stood from the couch. "Why don't we talk later when you've calmed down?"

He headed for the door.

"Where are you going?" Ali screeched. Her stomach suddenly flipped. "You're going to Colton's, aren't you? You're literally walking out on me and going to him!"

Otis turned the door handle and looked back over his shoulder at her. "Bye."

And with that, he headed through the door.

Ali grabbed his discarded computer console controller and threw it at him. It was too late. He closed the door and the controller crashed into it.

The damn thing didn't even break.

But Ali was determined to get her poetic justice somehow. She headed for the fridge and grabbed the champagne bottle stored there. There was no point letting the expensive bottle go to waste.

She held it up to the dingy lightbulb as condensation dripped down the side and onto her hand.

"To Otis!" she said, popping the cork.

It hit the ceiling with a dull thud and bounced back onto the tiled floor below. As the champagne inside the bottle fizzed up to the rim, Ali took a swig to stop it spilling over. Delicious bubbles danced across her tongue, forcing a rueful smile to inch across her lips.

She turned to the silent, empty apartment and held the bottle aloft.

"Let the commiseration party begin!"

CHAPTER THREE

"Sis, you're slurring so bad, I could've sworn you just said Otis is gay."

"I did," Ali hiccupped into her cell phone. She took another glug of champagne. She'd almost drained the entire thing.

"GAY," she said again, resting her forehead on the kitchen table. "G. A. Double Y."

On the other end of the line, her brother Teddy was completely silent. Finally, he let out a high-pitched exclamation.

"You know, he never set my gaydar off once. But I totally see it now you mention it. He has a swagger in his hips. And he's always with that Colton guy, who's as gay as pink lemonade. Oh…"

"Yeah," Ali said glumly. "Oh."

Teddy was always Ali's go-to when she needed support. You'd think it would be Hannah but ever since she'd become a hard, corporate type, trying to connect with her on an emotional level was like trying to get blood from a stone. Hannah had always been serious, even before their parents divorced. Their mom, Georgia, liked to joke that Hannah was born in a business suit, but Hannah didn't find it funny because Hannah didn't find anything funny.

Teddy, on the other hand, was a gregarious laugher, a free spirit, a fun seeker, the life and soul of every party. He was, quite simply, Ali's favorite human being on the planet.

"I'm so sorry, Ali-cat," he said, using the affectionate nickname he'd given her as a kid after she'd become obsessed with cats, which she still was to this day. "What are you going to do?"

"Well, Teddy-bear," Ali replied, using *his* pet name, whose origins were altogether more obvious. "I'm going to finish drinking this bottle of expensive champagne and then I'm going to give Otis's computer a bath." She let out a wry snort.

"Sounds like a solid plan," Teddy joked. "And after that? Is he moving out? Are you staying in the apartment? Are you going to keep living there? I mean, I know you can afford it on your own…"

He used a pointed tone. Teddy had always been particularly unimpressed with the way Otis loafed off of her, especially since Teddy was an aspiring actor himself and he'd worked every menial job under the sun to pay his way.

With the topic turning to work, Ali gasped. She'd been so sidetracked by Otis's bombshell, she'd completely forgotten about the other life-changing event she'd gone through that day.

She placed the champagne bottle down on the table clumsily, and it landed with a heavy-handed thud.

"That's the other thing," she said, feeling distinctly more sober. "I don't have a job anymore."

Teddy gasped. "What? Why? What happened?"

"The inevitable. I made the crème brûlée that broke the camel's back."

Teddy fell silent. "Hon. Is this the beginning of a spiral? I'm in Venice Beach at the moment but I can catch a cab if you need me."

"Oh please," Ali scoffed. "I'm not Hannah. I know it's unhealthy to suppress emotions. I don't spiral."

For all her successes in life, Hannah's emotional well-being left a lot to be desired. Their marathon-running, junk-food-abstaining, vitamin-popping sister could not be convinced that an hour a week with a therapist would do as much good for her health as the other three. More, probably, considering just how tightly wound she was.

"Then enlighten me," Teddy said. "Why has my absurdly talented little sister just quit a steady, handsomely paying job she'd trained hard for years to get? Training that used up her inheritance, as well, if I recall correctly."

When he put it that way, Ali did start to see how rash she'd been.

"Let me clarify," Ali began, finding her poise. "I got fired."

"That's worse!" Teddy exclaimed. "It'll look terrible on your CV! You'll never get another job as a pastry chef now."

"I don't want another job as a pastry chef," Ali told him, firmly. "I don't want to make crème brûlées every damn hour of every damn day. You said it yourself, I'm talented. I trained hard. I spent a ton of money. I'm more than just a crème brûlée girl!"

"I wish I was recording this," Teddy murmured. "Tell me. What are you?"

"I'm… I'm a pâtissier! I'm Milo Baptiste's protégé. I'm… I'm… unemployed."

The reality hit her just like that. She no longer had a job. Or an income. A wave of panic started rising through her.

"You're also single," Teddy added.

14

"Teddy!" Ali wailed. "Why would you say that?"

"Because it's true, and you're going to have to process it. You said yourself, you're no Hannah. In which case, you'd better let it all out."

He spoke in a soothing tone, but if he'd been physically present, Ali still would've smacked him.

"Get it all out of your system," he continued, sounding like a self-help guru.

Her emotions got the better of her. Tears spilled down her cheeks. She let out a stifled, hiccupping sob.

"There," Teddy said. "Don't you feel better for having gotten that out of your system?"

Ali sniffed. "A little."

"Good. Now tomorrow you can wake up as the fierce tigress you are and take on the world."

"You think I'm fierce?"

"The fiercest," Teddy told her.

"Thanks," she mumbled.

"What are you?" Teddy prompted.

"A tigress," she murmured.

"That's right. You're going to land on your feet. Now what's your goddamn plan, woman!"

"I don't have one yet."

"Do you have any savings?"

"No. But I'll get by. You do."

"I signed up for instability," he told her, sternly. "I'm built for it. You're not. That's why you studied hard and got a sensible job."

"Hey, didn't you have an audition today?" Ali asked, diverting the conversation for a much needed moment of respite.

"Ugh. Don't even. It was lousy," he said. "I definitely didn't get the part. According to the very straight director, in his pale jeans and backwards baseball cap, I didn't read gay enough. Me!" He let out a rueful laugh. "As if he was expecting a certain level of innate flamboyance. You know, because my actually being a gay man doesn't make me qualified enough to accurately portray one!"

"Maybe you should audition for Otis's gay sitcom in New York," Ali said, glumly.

Teddy paused. "Gay sitcom? In New York?" He gasped theatrically. "Don't tell me he landed a role on *Kweenz*."

"I don't know what it's called."

15

"Oh, hon. If he did, he is going to be a star and mark my words. You're a couple of months away from being the poor straight ex-lover of a gay superstar actor. He's going to talk about you in interviews. *'I loved her so much, but I couldn't keep living a lie,'* blah blah blah."

"Great," Ali said glumly. "I have that to look forward to."

"Now listen," Teddy said, suddenly sounding all business. "You have got to use this to your advantage. Sort your stuff out right this instant. Find your next step, your next path, and take this moment to shine. Quick fire. Don't think, just answer. What do you want to be? Go."

"A pâtissier."

He made the noise of an incorrect buzzer on a gameshow. "Wrong answer. You already blew that. Try again. Think bigger."

"Bigger? I mean, I guess I did always picture myself running my own bakery. Baking all the things I wanted to. Wearing pearls like Julia Child. Using my creativity like Milo taught me to. I could fill the menu with exquisite French pastries and I'd never have to make another crème brûlée!"

Teddy clapped. "There you go! Now hold on to that dream, sis. Hold on to it. Visualize it. We need to put it out into the universe."

The universe, Ali thought ruefully.

But she did as she was commanded. She closed her eyes and pictured herself as a business owner, standing proudly outside the doors of a gorgeous high-end bakery. The warm California sun shining down on her, an ocean breeze rippling through her blond braid. No, not braid. Her loose blond hair, with a perfect wave. She was her own manager. There was no Russell barking demands at her. No Otis taking her earnings. There was the dog she'd always wanted at her feet, and a hanging basket of pretty pink flowers, and a gorgeous hunky man with his top off...

"Can you see it?" came Teddy's voice in her ear.

"I can see it," she said dreamily.

"Wanna know how you make it happen?"

"Yes," she said, licking her lips at the sun-kissed golden skin of her dream heartthrob.

"Come to Willow Bay with me tomorrow."

Ali frowned. She opened her eyes. The gorgeous beach hunk of her dreams disappeared as she was transported back to her lonely apartment.

"Where?" she asked.

"Willow Bay. It's near Venice. There's this boardwalk I've never been to, full of new stores. Food stores. They're having a food festival tomorrow. You could do some networking. Ask for some advice."

"Networking?" Ali said with a grimace. "That sounds a bit *actorish*."

"Say you'll come. Step one of your new life. Please?"

Ali hesitated. It wasn't like she had anything better going on. No job. No boyfriend. May as well eat her way through her woes. That was step one to healing a broken heart, after all.

"Fine," she said. "What's the worst that could happen?"

CHAPTER FOUR

Whimsical was the first word that came to Ali's mind as her car crested the hill and the small town of Willow Bay opened up before her.

Like most California beach towns, it was surrounded by tree-covered hills. But the architecture wasn't like anything she'd seen before. At least not in California. The buildings were three and four stories high, like townhouses, with flat facades and huge windows. They were painted bright colors and had large wooden doors. In fact, it looked to Ali like every building had been transported there straight from Havana. The tall rainbow houses went all the way from the hills to the seafront, like a staircase for a giant toddler.

It was so quirky and unique, Ali thought it would make a good location for a film. Then she immediately shook away the thought. Films had actors. Otis was an actor. The last thing she wanted to think about right now was her ex-boyfriend.

She parked and exited her car, choosing instead to think about how nice it was to get out of the city for once. The haze and heat of LA could get a bit much sometimes, without the ocean air to blow away the car fumes. But in Willow Bay, the air was positively refreshing. And instead of the background hum of traffic, there was the gentle sound of surf against the shoreline, and the crooning of seagulls overhead.

Ali took a deep, relaxing breath. Even the sun against her skin felt less oppressive here. More like a caress than an assault of harsh UV rays.

She followed the palm tree–lined path down to the cove. Here, the golden sand was dotted with multicolored beach umbrellas for the sunbathers. Barefoot joggers zigzagged between them. A solitary artist sat on a stool painting the aquamarine water, which was calm enough for paddle boarding. There was even a gondola, Ali noticed with delight, amending her initial impression of Willow Bay as Havana, to Havana mixed with Italy.

To her right, there was a wooden archway with the words *Yacht Harbor* carved into it, and signs advertising fishing, boating, an aquarium, and a museum. In the other direction was a boardwalk brimming with colorful storefronts, which ran parallel to the beach. Coming off it was a pier filled with fairground rides.

Ali took a long, deep breath. Willow Bay was wonderful. A vibrant, buzzing, wholly unique place. She felt suddenly as if she was standing at the epicenter of the universe, in a place designed just for her.

Ali began walking along the boardwalk. She'd arranged to meet Teddy at the entrance to the food festival, and could see a cordoned off area in the distance of bright parasols and picnic tables and the billowing smoke of barbecues. As she strolled, she was pleasantly surprised to see there wasn't a single franchise store in sight. Every store she passed was independent, selling everything from tacky tourist souvenirs to vintage clothes, fried donuts to little pots of steaming clam chowder. It was a real mix, and everything was unified with a joyful energy.

Ali reached the entrance to the food festival and sniffed the amazing aromas of barbecue ribs, pulled pork, and rotisserie chicken. She was glad Teddy had cajoled her into this. It beat sitting at home wallowing in her misery.

As Ali leaned against the railings to wait for Teddy, a couple walked past her into the festival, hand in hand, with big, smug smiles plastered onto their faces.

Give it three years, Ali thought. *See how smug you feel when you can't pry his eyes away from his computer games.*

Her gaze roved across the pretty wooden beach houses. Families sat around fold-out tables in swimwear and with sopping wet hair. Happy families always intrigued Ali. Not that hers was exceptionally messy, but they'd never be able to peacefully visit a beach together like that.

Hannah's kids would be tearing up the place for starters, while her anxiety-prone husband, Jackson, tried his best to preempt every trip or spill they might make—something he always failed at, which only served to rile his children further and disappoint his wife all at the same time. Then her mom would find something to complain about—too hot, too windy, not enough shade, too many seagulls—and then there'd be the ever-present unspoken absence of her father. In a nutshell, it would be fraught.

The shrill ring of her phone brought Ali out of her ruminations. Teddy's name flashed on the screen. He was probably calling to tell her he was running late. That was very typical of her big brother.

She answered the call. "Let me guess, you're stuck on the I-10. You'll be fifteen minutes, but actually thirty, so I may as well do a recce and scout out a spot for lunch. Am I close?"

"Ish," Teddy said.

"Which bit did I get wrong?"

"The I-10 bit."

"Teddy!" Ali exclaimed. "Are you not even on the I-10 yet?"

"Bingo."

"Where are you?" she huffed.

"West Hollywood."

"And what the heck are you doing there?"

"I have an audition," Teddy explained. "My agent called me an hour ago. It's all been very last minute. Apparently the super straight director from yesterday thought I might be suitable for a role in his friend's show, and passed on my details. I'm so sorry. I'll come as soon as it's over."

"How long will that be?"

"Honestly, sis, I don't know. A few hours. Will you forgive me?"

"Yes, obviously," Ali said, though she was a bit put out. Being ditched by two guys for auditions, two days in a row, put something of a dent in her ego. "But what am I going to do in the meantime? And don't say scout out a place for lunch. That's not going to kill a few hours, is it?"

"Walk on the beach. Swim. Flirt with a paddle boarder. I don't know. Use your imagination."

"All right, all right," Ali said. Teddy could be trying sometimes. "Good luck with your audition. I mean, break a leg. Whatever."

"Thanks."

The call ended. Ali stared at the cell phone in her hand, then sighed and shoved it deep inside her pocket. She peered around, squinting against the glare of the sun. Her gaze fell to the pier, and the fairground rides and arcades dotted along it. Perhaps it wouldn't be so hard to kill a few hours after all.

*

The entrance of the pier was flanked on either side by fast food kiosks. The smells of sugary donuts and greasy fries mingled deliciously in the air.

Ali paused and sniffed the aromas.

"Watch your back!" a voice cried.

Ali turned just in time for a roller skater in nothing but tight Speedos to streak past her in a blur. The wheels of his skates made a rhythmic beat on the wooden planks of the pier. Ali smiled, and took her first step onto the wooden boards.

She strolled slowly, letting the ocean air stir her hair. She reached a carousel. It was designed to look like a traditional French one, with gaudily painted horses. Creepy circus music played through its speakers as the carousel turned round and round with a couple of chubby toddlers squealing with delight.

Beyond the carousel was a mini children's roller coaster. The train was designed to look like a bright pink worm, with a tunnel shaped like a big red apple.

Right at the end of the pier stood a yellow Ferris wheel. It had a distinctly '90s feel to its design and color scheme, with large patches of rust blemishing the mechanism and carts. Ali could picture it in its heyday, pristine and swarming with kids with side ponytails and high-top sneakers.

But no sooner had Ali conjured the image of it in her mind's eye than she suddenly realized it wasn't her imagination at all. It was a memory. She'd been here before! *She'd* been the kid with a side ponytail and high-top sneakers!

Ali couldn't remember when exactly she'd stood at this very spot, but the memory was strong, vivid, and full of nostalgia. The seagulls soaring through the sky behind the Ferris wheel, the flashing lights, even the creepy fairground music was the same. And she could remember she was holding hands with her father.

It all came back to Ali in a sudden rush, a long forgotten memory resurfacing as vivid as if it had happened yesterday. Her tugging on her dad's hand, leading him across the pier to the Ferris wheel, desperate to ride it. She couldn't have been much older than ten because she'd stopped holding hands with him around that age. She remembered that clearly, because shortly after, her parents had divorced, and she'd always wondered if he'd taken it as a sign that she didn't need him anymore. Of course, she knew now, as an adult woman, that relationships were significantly more complicated than that. But the ten-year-old inside of her couldn't let that thought go. And it was so far from the truth. She'd never stopped needing him, even though his phone calls became less and less frequent, even though she'd raged at him as a teenager because he was never physically there and a disembodied voice on a phone couldn't substitute for the real thing, and even when she gave him the cold shoulder at graduation because he'd let a whole year lapse without calling and hadn't even sent a birthday card. She even needed him now, even though years had passed since he'd contacted her and she was full of bitter rage. Perhaps if he was here now, she'd feel less unmoored. Perhaps her breakup wouldn't hurt so much if she had a cuddle from her dad for comfort. Perhaps being unemployed wouldn't be so scary with her dad there to tell her everything would be okay.

At that very moment, Ali saw a man waving at her. Her heart stopped.

It was him. It was her dad.

CHAPTER FIVE

Ali couldn't believe her eyes. Her heart soared. She went flying along the pier, toward the Ferris wheel, waving at her father.

But as she got a little closer, her hopes were dashed. The man was not her father at all. He couldn't be. He was too young, at forty-something, the age she remembered him being, rather than the sixty-odd he would be now.

Disappointed, Ali drew to a halt. She watched as a young blond girl—the girl the man was actually waving at—hurried up to him and took his hand.

They headed for the Ferris wheel together, hand in hand, just as Ali and her dad had done all those years ago. Ali couldn't help but wonder if the same fate that had befallen her was on this child's horizon. She got the urge to run over and cry, "Don't trust him! He'll let you down!" but she held herself back, because in all likelihood, this child's father would be a better man than hers.

"The one you love is closer than you think," a voice suddenly whispered in Ali's ear.

Ali jumped. She turned her head sharply over her shoulder and came face to face with a rhesus macaque.

The monkey blinked at her, with disconcertingly human mischief in its eyes.

Ali screeched and staggered back. "What did you just say?"

The macaque cackled and darted back, revealing it was standing on the shoulder of a woman.

The woman gazed at Ali with soft, mysterious eyes of a brilliant emerald green. The long black wavy hair that trailed down her back was adorned with colored threads and beads.

Recovering at last from her shock, Ali took in the woman from head to toe. She was dressed in a vibrantly patterned skirt that reached right down to her toes, and a white cropped peasant top with puffed sleeves. The macaque on her shoulder was also wearing clothes—a little red waist coat stitched with gold, and matching bloomers, like the ringleader of a circus. All that was missing was a top hat.

Ali grimaced. This woman was probably panhandling, using a cute monkey as a gimmick to get more cash off the tourists. Ali herself had no patience for people who kept wild animals as pets, especially ones who dressed them up like mini humans.

The woman batted her long black lashes at Ali and smiled. It wasn't a particularly pleasant smile. There was an eeriness to it.

"The one you love is closer than you think," she said again, her European accent like honey in Ali's ears. Then she gestured with her jewelry-adorned hand toward a wagon.

It was a proper Romani caravan, painted dark green with a swirling floral motif on the side. A set of wooden stairs led up to the doors. Painted above them in an arc were the words *Lavinia Leigh. LOVE. LIFE. LUCK.*

A fortune teller, Ali thought, dispassionately. *Just what I need.*

Ali had no time for the world of tarot cards and clairvoyance. To her, fortune tellers were just people with a knack for spotting the emotionally vulnerable and telling them some generic information that could apply to at least half the population. It didn't take a genius to work out that a slightly forlorn-looking thirty-something woman was going through a breakup.

"I don't need my fortune told," she told the woman sharply.

The macaque yipped.

"Are you sure?" Lavinia asked, tickling her monkey under the chin. "Because Django seems to think you do."

Ali had to stop herself from snorting her distaste. She was even less inclined to listen to a fortune teller who pretended her pet monkey was some kind of empath!

"I'm pretty sure Django doesn't give a crap about me," Ali replied, coolly. "I'm just waiting for someone."

"Your father," Lavinia said.

The word hit Ali like a freight train. Her eyes widened.

"What? Why did you say that?" she demanded.

Lavinia said nothing. She merely gestured once again to her caravan.

Ali folded her arms.

"I'm not going in there," she said, stubbornly.

Just then, Django the macaque sprang onto Ali's shoulder and started clambering all over her like some kind of spider. As much as Ali loved animals, she wasn't particularly thrilled to have a monkey scrabbling around in her hair.

23

"Can you get the monkey off me?" Ali asked, feeling him settle on the top of her head like some kind of hat.

Lavinia shrugged. "Django has chosen you."

Ali rolled her eyes. She knew how this went. The only way the monkey would get off was if she agreed to let the woman tell her fortune.

"Fine," she sighed, admitting defeat. "I'll take the reading."

Just like that, Django bounded off her head and back onto the fortune teller's shoulder.

He grinned, baring his pointy little fangs.

Ali patted down her tangled hair and straightened her rumpled clothes.

"After you," Lavinia said, calmly, gesturing with her arm toward the open door of the caravan.

Reluctantly, Ali clomped up the wooden steps.

It was dark inside the caravan, which was lit only by a couple of candles. The small space smelled strongly of incense and varnished wood, though not strongly enough to cover up the aroma of Django's urine.

The monkey scurried past Ali and leapt through the open doors of a cage. He started swinging back and forth on a swing inside.

"Take a seat," came Lavinia's voice from behind.

Ali flopped down onto the wooden stool, and the woman inched past, crouching so as not to hit her head on the ornate brass oil lamp hanging from the ceiling.

"How much is this going to cost me?" Ali asked.

"You've already paid," Lavinia said, mysteriously, taking the seat opposite her.

Ali decided not to press it. If this crazy woman wanted to tell her fortune for free, then fine. She had a few hours to kill anyway.

"Where are your tarot cards?" Ali asked, looking at the blank tabletop between them.

"I'm a psychic," Lavinia said. "I don't use cards. I just need to tune into your frequency."

Ali raised an eyebrow. Her frequency? Really? This whole thing was *so* Teddy. He swore by horoscopes and signs, vibrations and auras, crystals and tarot cards. To Ali, all that stuff was laughably ridiculous.

"Your brother's running late again," Lavinia said.

Ali frowned. A lucky guess. Because no one was ever on time with the LA traffic the way it was.

"Wow," Ali said. "I guess you're legit after all."

Lavinia just smiled. "You're in pain."

Again, you didn't have to be a psychic to notice Ali's eyes were still puffy from yesterday's crying.

"Willow Bay wants to heal you," Lavinia announced.

"Does it?" Ali asked, sarcastically. "How does it intend to do that?"

Lavinia opened her arms wide. "Everything you need is right here. If you look, it will provide. It's up to you whether you take this gift."

"Right," Ali said, leaning forward on her elbows. "Here's something you can tell me. How bad is the traffic on the I-10 right now? I'd like to know how long I have left to kill."

"Your brother isn't far," Lavinia replied.

"Could you maybe narrow it down to five minutes?" Ali asked.

Lavinia sat back and laid her hands on the table. She was kind of pretty, Ali realized now, albeit in a creepy way, like a porcelain doll from the Victorian era.

"You're a skeptic," she said.

"I'm just waiting for the good stuff," Ali replied. "Tall dark stranger. Come into some money. Jupiter aligning with Mars. Yadda yadda yadda."

From his perch in the corner, Django began to cackle.

A crooked smile flitted across Lavinia's lips. The fortune teller leaned forward on her elbows, getting uncomfortably close to Ali. Her green eyes seemed to bore into her.

Ali gulped.

Finally, Lavinia sat back. "Your problem is that you always know what you'll get at the end because you are always following the same recipe."

Ali hesitated. Even she had to admit that was kinda spooky. There was nothing about her outward appearance that would give a clue as to her profession. Lavinia had somehow found the only metaphor that would speak to Ali.

"You must change the recipe," Lavinia continued. "You've done the same thing over and over again, with the same outcome over and over again. But change just one ingredient, and something you never expected may result."

Now Ali was getting thoroughly creeped out. Her mind went to her crème brûlées, to the robotic actions she made them with. The same thing. Over and over. The same outcome. Over and over. Then the one time it was different, the one time the spearmint had three leaves

25

instead of four, it had started this whole chain of events. Her job. Otis. Even being here in Willow Bay. She could draw a line right back to that sprig of spearmint.

"Different isn't bad," Lavinia continued. "In fact, different is rarely the catastrophe we expect it to be. That small change is, instead, an opportunity. A reminder to blaze your own trail. To be creative. And once you become creative, the recipe is no longer a set of rules to follow, but a journey to walk upon, adding different flavors, techniques, trying different quantities, adjusting, playing. All the answers are right here, waiting for you." She smiled. "You might want to get that."

Ali's phone started to ring. She jumped, thoroughly freaked out.

She retrieved it from her purse. Teddy was calling her.

"I told you the traffic wasn't that bad," Lavinia said.

Without a word, Ali stood and rushed out of the caravan into the bright California sunshine. Her hands were shaking as she answered her phone. Teddy's voice filled her ear.

"Sis, I'm literally almost there. Just parking now. Did you find somewhere to eat?"

"Not yet," Ali murmured. She was still freaked out from what Lavinia had said. It had really given her the heebie-jeebies.

"Good, because I have a hankering for Italian," Teddy continued. "So look for a pizzeria."

"Pizza. Got it."

She scanned the boardwalk ahead of her, spotting not one but two pizzerias, either side of a vacant store. One was called Marco's. The other Emilio's.

"Found one," she announced.

"Fab," Teddy said. "By the way, I left my wallet at home. Can you spot me for lunch?"

"Lemme check." She reached into her pocket and pulled out a folded up twenty. "Yeah. I can spot you."

Then she paused. There'd also been a ten in there earlier. Definitely. She'd taken it out of the battered cookie tin Otis used as a piggy bank to save for his computer games.

Suddenly, Ali realized what had happened to her missing ten-dollar bill.

"That monkey!" she cried.

She swirled on the spot and glared at the caravan. That's what Lavinia had meant when she said she'd already paid; Django had pickpocketed her!

"Great," Teddy said, "I'll be there in five."

The call ended, and Ali headed toward the two pizzerias to see which was cheaper. But the closer she got, the more her attention went to the vacant store between them.

Ali immediately recalled her drunken chat with Teddy the night before, and the bakery he'd told her to visualize. The dream he'd told her to put out into the universe. Could this be the universe responding? Was this what Lavinia Leigh meant when she said that everything she needed was right here? That if she looked, it would be provided?

She hurried toward the store. There was even a hanging basket by the door, just like the one she'd imagined—only it wasn't filled with the pretty pink flowers of Ali's dreams, but dead, dry, burned to a crisp ones. Still, it was similar enough to send a shiver down Ali's spine.

Then Ali shook herself. She was being absurd. She'd never be able to actually open her own bakery. She didn't have the money, for starters.

Lavinia Leigh may think a change in ingredients was in order, but Ali knew there was just no chance she'd ever be able to make her dream a reality. It just wasn't written in her stars.

CHAPTER SIX

Teddy arrived in a fluster, his strawberry-blond curls plastered to his forehead with sweat. His chubby cheeks were flushed pink, the same color as his boating shorts.

"Ali-cat!" he cried across the pizzeria. "I'm so sorry I'm late!"

Teddy never shied away from making a spectacle. Luckily for the more reserved Ali, she was the only customer in the place.

Her brother blustered toward her—Teddy always moved like he was in a perpetual hurricane—and air kissed her cheeks. Then he plonked himself into the seat opposite her and helped himself to a swig of her water.

"I'm parched," he exclaimed, fanning his face with a menu, glancing around at his surroundings in a manner reminiscent of a meerkat. "Did you order?"

It always took Ali a bit of time to recalibrate herself when Teddy was around. It was like the world moved at a faster speed and she had to jog to keep up. It could be quite exhausting sometimes.

"I got us a classic margherita to share," she said with a smile. "Is that okay?"

"Perfect," Teddy said, slapping his palms on the tabletop with a flourish.

He was in a good mood then.

"I take it the audition went well," Ali suggested.

Teddy shrugged. "Honestly, it's hard to tell. It was quick, which could mean they hated me so much they didn't want to see any more. But they didn't cut me off mid-monologue and tell me to leave, so maybe it was quick because they liked me so much they didn't need to see more. The important thing is that my acting was on point. I should turn up to all my auditions underprepared."

As he spoke, Ali squinted at him. Something had changed. His teeth. They looked... kind of blue.

"What have you done to your teeth?" she asked.

Teddy ran his tongue along them. "I whitened them for a toothbrush commercial."

"That's supposed to be white?"

Teddy laughed. "I know, they're a bit alarming. But you know what they say about the camera."

"That it adds ten pounds?" Ali quipped.

"Well yes. But also you can get away with a heck of a lot more makeup. And, apparently, blue teeth. Point is, it'll look absolutely fine on screen."

"Well, just be careful when you're out and about at night," Ali said with a smirk. "I bet those things glow in the dark."

Just then, the server approached their table. He had a tray perched on the tips of his fingers like a pro. He looked like the archetypal Italian man, with dark, wavy hair, tanned skin, and a chiseled jawline sporting perfectly sculpted stubble. He moved with suave confidence, with elegance, presenting their pizza like it was part of a dance.

Ali's mouth watered. Not just because of the gorgeous specimen of a man standing beside her, but because of the fresh, doughy margherita pizza in front of her and the wonderful aroma of fresh basil billowing into her face.

"This looks fantastic," Teddy said, his eyes widening with hunger. "Emilio, is it?"

"*Marco,*" the man corrected. "Emilio's is the other store."

"The one on the other side of the vacant lot?" Ali asked with interest. She thought of the store, the perfect spot for her bakery.

"Yes," Marco confirmed. Then whispered, "The overpriced one."

Ali got the distinct impression the two pizza joints were rivals. She briefly entertained the thought of being sandwiched in the middle of two warring Italians. If Emilio was as gorgeous as Marco, that wouldn't be a bad thing.

"We'll make sure never to go there," Teddy told Marco with a wink.

Marco nodded, satisfied, and returned to the kitchen.

Teddy grabbed a slice of glistening pizza. "I'm famished." He took a huge bite with his blue-white teeth. Then, through his mouthful, he asked, "Why did you shout 'monkey' when we were on the phone earlier?"

Ali frowned. "Huh?"

"Earlier. When we were talking. I asked if you could spot me for lunch, and you shouted "monkey!""

His impression of her was spot on.

Ali's mind went to Django, the pickpocketing macaque. She wasn't sure whether telling Teddy about the fortune teller was a good idea. He'd only make a thing out of it.

She grabbed a slice of pizza.

"There was a monkey on the pier," she said evasively, before shoving her pizza into her mouth to avoid having to answer any follow-up questions.

"That's a bit weird," Teddy replied through a mouthful of greasy cheese. "Was it someone's pet?"

Ali chewed and chewed, giving a shrug as her answer. The pizza was absolutely delicious.

"Was it wearing clothes?" Teddy continued.

"Uh-huh," Ali said, still chewing away.

"So it was definitely a pet. I mean the only people I know who'd ever keep a monkey as a pet would be a fortune teller or something." He stopped, his eyes widened. "No way! Ali-cat, did you go and speak to a fortune teller?"

Damn, Ali thought. He had the sort of power of deduction Lavinia Leigh would be proud of!

She swallowed her mouthful. "Yes. But don't go getting all over-excited about it. It was a one-off to kill time."

Too late. Teddy had started flapping his hands excitedly. "Tell me everything! How did you even meet a fortune teller, because I don't believe for a second you had your fortune told of your own free will."

Ali sighed and put her pizza slice down. There was no getting out of it. She'd have to spill.

"I was standing by the Ferris wheel on the pier and I suddenly remembered that we'd been here before. When we were kids. With Dad."

There was an instantaneous change in Teddy's demeanor. He didn't like to talk about their father. Their parents' divorce had happened not long after Teddy had come out, and he'd never been able to shake the insecurity that he'd caused it, in the same way Ali couldn't shake her fear that ceasing to hold her dad's hand had caused it.

"Oh yeah, sure, years ago," Teddy replied, stiffly.

"So I was looking at the Ferris wheel, and I saw a guy who looked just like him. Dad, I mean. But obviously it wasn't, 'cause this guy was in his forties."

"Uh-huh," Teddy said, shifting uncomfortably in his seat.

30

Ali hurried it along. "Just as I was looking at this man, a voice said in my ear, 'The one you love is closer than you know.' So I turned and there was this monkey."

Teddy frowned. "Are you sure it was just champagne you had yesterday?"

"It was the fortune teller," Ali explained. "The monkey was on her shoulder. Then he stole my money and sat on my head until I agreed to have my fortune told."

Teddy chuckled. "I'm just imagining you with a monkey for a hat. So? What's the verdict?"

Now it was Ali's turn to shift awkwardly. The whole experience with Lavinia had really shaken her to the core. For whatever reason, she just couldn't get over it, over the cooking metaphor and how perfectly it correlated with her life.

"She seemed to think that Willow Bay would provide me with all the answers I was looking for," Ali said.

"Interesting," Teddy said. "What else?"

"And that if I keep cooking the same recipe, I'll always get the same outcome, but if I take a risk and change it, I might not always be right, but it won't be the catastrophe I expect."

She thought again of the sprig of spearmint that had set off this whole string of events.

"And?" Teddy prompted.

"And then I left the pier and saw a vacant store. Like right away. I hadn't noticed it before, but it was right there."

Teddy's eyes widened. "Signs!" he exclaimed.

"I knew you'd say that," Ali replied. "So I thought about how yesterday I'd told you about my dream of running a bakery. And I thought about how Otis is gone and my job is gone, but it's not anywhere near as bad as I was expecting."

"Are you seriously telling me you found something a fortune teller said useful?"

"I know. Weird, huh?"

Teddy grew animated. "Ali, you have to go for it."

She shook her head. As much as she'd love to, relocating and starting her own business felt like far too much on top of everything she was going through.

"I can't," she said. "Starting a business is so risky. Especially a food one. Do you know how many businesses make it to their second year? It's something crazy like two percent!"

31

Teddy gave her a serious look. "You think anyone's going to want to hire you after your little crème brûlée mishap? This might be your only option."

Ali didn't appreciate his doomy attitude. She was stressed enough about all the changes that had happened recently, she didn't need him piling on more anxiety.

"I don't have the money," she told him, firmly. It was best to nip this in the bud.

"I can lend you some."

"You?" Ali replied, barking out a laugh. "Since when did you have any money to spare?"

Teddy pointed to his blue-white teeth. "Since my toothpaste commercial."

Ali paused. She hadn't actually expected Teddy to have any means to help her.

"I can't just take your money. You barely earn a thing."

"Which is more than you earn, sis," Teddy added. "Since you made yourself unemployed."

He took a huge bite of pizza, leaving Ali to stew in her reality. He was right. She'd basically burned all her bridges when she'd exploded a crème brûlée in front of a Hollywood executive. Getting a job in LA would be out of the question now. Relocating for work was almost a given. But that didn't solve the issue of the fact that Russell would be the one giving her a reference, one Ali already knew would be far from glowing.

So Teddy might be right about opening her own business being her only option. But that brought a whole new host of challenges and hurdles with it. Ali wouldn't even know where to begin with the venture.

"How about this..." Teddy said, wiping the grease from his lips with a napkin. "You show me this store, and we can have a little role play."

"Teddy," Ali interrupted, unenthused, "I'm not an actor. I don't role play my way through situations."

"Well, I am, and I do," he replied, sounding uppity. "Come on. I want to see my little sister's dreams come true, even if it's just imaginary."

Ali smiled. She couldn't help herself. Even when Teddy was pushing her buttons, he did it out of love. And even though running her own bakery could never happen, it would be fun to entertain the idea, even if it was just a fantasy role play.

"Fine, you twisted my arm," Ali said.

"Yay!" Teddy exclaimed. Then he paused and gestured to their half-eaten pizza. "We're going to finish this first though, right?"

CHAPTER SEVEN

Ali and Teddy stood side by side with their noses pressed against the window of the vacant storefront. Inside, the place was in disarray. The large counter was covered in debris. The tiled floor was covered in dust. There were metal brackets on the walls where shelves had once been, and wires hung from the ceiling where the light fixtures had been removed.

"It's not a lot to look at, is it?" Teddy said.

He moved back from the window. A smear of dirt had transferred from the glass onto his nose.

"Oh, you have a…" Ali began, but she was interrupted by Teddy's hysterical laughter.

His shoulders shook with amusement as he pointed a finger in her face. Presumably, she had her own nose-smudge. She rubbed it with her palm.

Teddy wiped away his own smudge.

"Okay," he said, all business. "Let's get into character." He shook himself, like an athlete about to start a race. "You're the world-famous protégé of Milo Baptiste, and I'm your agent."

Ali laughed. "You do know real people don't have agents, right?"

"Fine. Lawyer." He tapped the window, where a handwritten note was stuck to the inside, and wiggled his strawberry-blond brows. "The landlord's number. Shall we give him a call?"

"No!" Ali cried. "That's stepping way over the line of role play! *Way* over."

"It's called method acting," Teddy informed her. "Come on, Ali-cat. Take a risk."

Ali wasn't loving this. But she gave in with a reluctant nod. Teddy would never drop it otherwise.

She retrieved her cell phone from her pocket. Teddy nodded encouragingly as she typed in the landlord's digits from the window notice. She hit the green button and listened to the dial tone, shooting Teddy a *so-there* look.

He smirked.

The call connected.

"Yes?" a harried male voice asked.

It sounded to Ali like she'd disturbed him in the middle of something very important. She immediately regretted having caved to Teddy's pressure. But it was too late to back out now.

"I'm calling about the vacant store in Willow Bay," Ali said, her stomach swilling with nerves.

"You are?" the man trilled, suddenly enthusiastic. His accent was distinctly Irish. "Grand. Do you want to view it? Is today okay? I live just up the hill, so I can meet you whenever."

Ali immediately started panicking. That was not the response she'd been expecting!

She covered the speaker with her hand and shot an appealing glance at Teddy.

"He wants to arrange a viewing!" she whisper-cried. "Now!"

Teddy just gave her two thumbs up.

"Are you the pair standing outside now?" she heard the Irish man say in her ear.

She glanced about, alarmed.

"He can see us!" she whispered to Teddy.

"Uh… yes…" Ali said uncertainty.

"Thought so. I can see you from my house. I'm the yellow one up the hill behind the store."

The call cut out.

Ali craned her head around the store, glancing up the long street that stretched into the hillsides. Sure enough, a man was bustling out the front door of a canary yellow house barely a football field's distance away from where she was standing. He'd be here in a matter of minutes.

Ali's panic intensified. This was starting to run away with her, like a train with no brakes.

She widened her eyes at Teddy. "He's on his way!"

Teddy simply cracked his knuckles, getting himself into his self-appointed role as lawyer.

Ali glowered at him. "I love you, but sometimes I really hate you."

She felt extremely uncomfortable for roping this poor innocent man into their fantasy role play. There couldn't have been much interest in the place if he was willing to come running out of his house the second someone called. The wheels were in motion, and there was no backing

35

out now. Ali had been forced onto a roller coaster and was approaching the first peak, with no option but to plunge into the abyss.

The man was close enough now for Ali to hear his plodding footsteps. He started waving. Ali gave a small, limp wave in return.

He was short and tubby, with a nervous energy that reminded Ali of Winnie-the-Pooh. He was the sort of person who didn't walk but blustered.

"Kerrigan," he said in his bright Irish accent, as soon as the distance between them was small enough for his voice to carry. "Kerrigan O'Neal."

He hop-skipped the final few steps and held one hand out to Ali, while the other rummaged in his pocket for his keys.

"Ali Sweet," she said, shaking his small, rubbery hand.

"Sweet?" he repeated. "What a wonderful name."

"Thanks," Ali replied.

Kerrigan looked at Teddy. The Irish man had a permanent look of bemusement on his eyebrows, like his mind was elsewhere, reliving some perplexing memory. "And this is?"

"My bro—" Ali began.

But Teddy interjected.

"—Broker," he said. "Financial broker. And advisor. And lawyer. Ms. Sweet is considering many different venues for her new pastry venture. If she chooses Willow Bay it will bring significant money into the local economy."

Kerrigan looked slightly intimidated. "Right you are."

He turned to the door, jammed his key in the lock, and began wiggling it. It was clearly putting up some resistance. His cheeks started to go red as he pushed the door with his shoulder.

Suddenly, the key turned, and Kerrigan went staggering inside.

Ali and Teddy exchanged a glance, then followed him in.

"It's in need of a good clean," Kerrigan said, completely ignoring his earlier mishap. "But it's only a bit of superficial work."

Ali hardly heard him. His voice seemed to fade away as she glanced about her at the wonderful store.

It was very bright, thanks to the huge windows overlooking the ocean, and the dust they'd stirred on entering sparkled like glitter in the sunlight. The floor was tiled, like a diner, in a checkerboard pattern of peppermint green and white. The wooden counter was painted eggshell blue. Beside it was a glass-fronted display refrigerator, the type you'd find in a deli or an ice cream parlor. There wasn't much in the way of furniture, but the three leftover bistro tables were in a cute, rustic style, and the same pleasing, soft pastel palette as the rest of the store. One wall was taken up by a large floor to ceiling shelving unit of white-painted wood. It looked distinctly hand crafted.

Kerrigan was right about the needed work being superficial. A few more tables, and a thorough clean, and this place would be good to go.

A crackle of excitement ran through Ali's veins. She spun on the spot, lost in her imagination as she pictured how the place could be.

She visualized the display fridge full of French pastries—madeleines, croissants, and profiteroles—and herself behind it, filling up a cardboard box for a customer and her children. She pictured the wooden shelves full of trinkets and merchandise, like Milo Baptiste's cookbooks. No. *Her* cookbooks; she'd always dreamed of writing a bestselling recipe book one day, so why not picture that instead of Milo's? She added some happy customers to the tables—a French couple exclaiming how her pastries were the best they'd tasted outside of Paris—and a whole table of hunky, topless, bronzed surfers.

Then finally she looked out to the sea, to the pier. She pictured her ten-year-old self, in her high-top sneakers and side ponytail riding the Ferris wheel with her dad.

Suddenly, a feeling hit Ali that she'd not felt since before her father had left. The feeling of home.

Standing here, in this store, she felt at home for the first time in years. She felt like she was where she was always meant to be. Suddenly, those three years she'd wasted working at Éclairs and living with Otis felt like a momentary blip. This was where her life was meant to be.

"I'll take it," she blurted, spinning from the window to face Teddy and Kerrigan.

Kerrigan's bushy white eyebrows shot halfway up his forehead. Teddy's mouth dropped wide open. Ali must've really shocked him because it took a lot for Teddy to break character.

"Are you sure, Ali—Ms. Sweet?" Teddy said, stumbling over his words as he struggled to get back into his financial advisor-cum-lawyer persona. "We do have a lot of other viewings today."

The emphasis in his tone was not lost on Ali. He was telling her to slow down. To think about it. But Ali didn't need to. She hadn't felt this confident about anything in… well, forever!

"I'm certain," Ali told him firmly. "This is the place. I mean, as long as we still have the backing of the toothpaste … investors."

She wanted to give Teddy the chance to change his mind about his generous offer of donating his toothpaste commercial earnings to her venture.

"Absolutely," Teddy replied with a resolute nod. "The toothpaste investors want nothing more than to see your business thrive."

He grinned supportively, and Ali grinned her gratitude in return.

Teddy turned to Kerrigan.

"Let's talk money," he said coolly.

He gestured to one of the bistro tables, looking so businesslike, he'd give Hannah a run for her money.

Everyone sat.

Teddy steepled his hands on the table in front of him and peered at Kerrigan. "How much are you asking for?"

"It's five thousand a month," Kerrigan replied.

Shocked, Ali snapped her face to Teddy. Five *thousand* dollars? That would mean the entirety of his toothpaste commercial earnings would be gone in just one month's rent!

Teddy's expression remained impassive, though there was a slight stress twitch under his left eye that no amount of acting could hide from Ali's perceptive gaze.

"That's all in, I assume," Teddy said. "Bills, property tax... and obviously you'll have the place refurbished. It's clearly not fit for purpose in this state."

Kerrigan scratched his neck awkwardly. "Actually, the five grand is just the rent. That's what Pete, the last tenant, paid."

"Oh," Teddy said, blandly. He went to stand.

Kerrigan made a panicked gesture with his hands. "But we could waive some of the fees, if need be."

Teddy slowly sank back to sitting. "My client isn't interested in hidden fees. One straight up payment per month. Those are the terms. Take them or leave them."

Kerrigan worried his hands in his lap. But Teddy obviously had him. There couldn't have been much interest in the store for him to even be considering such a discount.

"Y—yes, I'm sure we can make that work," Kerrigan said.

"And the first month will be waived?" Teddy continued. "Because my client will need to buy all her equipment. It's simply not possible for her to use the space as it is."

"Y—yes, I suppose that's fine," Kerrigan said.

Teddy clapped his hands. "Then let's seal this deal, shall we? Would you like my lawyers to draw up the contract, or do you have one prepared?"

Kerrigan reached into his satchel. "I have one here. If it's acceptable to you, Ms. Sweet?"

Ali didn't possess the same acting skills as Teddy. She had to bite her lip to stop from screaming out with excitement.

"Yes," she said, trying to sound aloof. "That is… acceptable."

Kerrigan pushed the document across the table to Ali and placed a pen on top. Ali's cheeks became hotter and hotter. She could feel Teddy watching her out of the corner of her eye as she picked up the pen and turned to the first page of the agreement.

"Maybe we should look at this back at home—I mean, the office?" Ali said.

"I can assure you the toothpaste investors are on board," Teddy urged.

Ali took a deep breath and signed on the dotted line.

CHAPTER EIGHT

Panic set in the moment Kerrigan left Ali and Teddy on the sidewalk of the store, with the signed agreement tucked under his arm and a set of keys deposited in Ali's hand.

"Did I really just do that?" Ali squealed to Teddy.

"Yup," Teddy replied with a grin.

It had all happened so quickly. She'd gotten carried away in the moment, caught up in play acting a rich, famous chef with a personal financial broker. But now, back in the light of day, when she was plain old Ali Sweet with no savings, it started to dawn on her what she'd actually just done.

"Is it too late to back out?" Ali said, freaking out.

Teddy looked at the keys in her hands. "Yeah, I'm pretty sure it's too late now."

"Where am I doing to live?" Ali said, suddenly thinking of all the practical things she'd blithely ignored while caught up in her role play. "I can't commute from LA every day."

"Already covered," Teddy said, wiggling his eyebrows.

Confused, Ali frowned. Teddy pointed to another notice in the window of the store. This one was advertising a studio apartment. *Small one bed, one bath, kitchen-diner, beachside.*

Ali glanced over at the multicolored stone cottages along the shore that the ad must be referring to. They were all squished in together, with no road outside, just a footpath to connect them.

"In one of the rainbow houses?" she said.

Now she really did start freaking out about it all. The serendipity of it all made her stomach turn somersaults. She thought of the fortune teller on the pier, and her prediction that Willow Bay would provide. It certainly seemed to be doing just that.

"Shall we give them a call?" Teddy prompted.

"I guess we better," Ali replied.

She grabbed her phone and began typing in the number. But as she did, her phone helpfully told her she'd dialed the number before. It was Kerrigan O'Neal's number.

Ali looked up at Teddy. "You're never going to believe this!"

*

Ali felt rather awkward as the bumbling man came all the way back down the hill just a moment after they'd sent him up it.

"I didn't think to mention the apartment," he said as he jiggled around for another set of keys lost to the depths of his pockets. "I assumed Ms. Sweet would want a bigger property."

Without missing a beat, Teddy said, "This is just for her guests."

Kerrigan nodded like that made perfect sense, and opened the door. Behind his back, Ali flashed Teddy a look. Sometimes the ease with which he lied alarmed her. And how would she keep up this ridiculous charade, considering Kerrigan O'Neal was potentially going to be her landlord twice over?

But as she stepped inside the little apartment, all of Ali's thoughts and concerns melted away. The place was small, but very charming, and with a lovely view of the ocean. It was the perfect size for her—the bedroom was large enough for a double bed and wardrobe, there was no bath but the shower looked decently sized, and the kitchen area at one side of the living room would be adequate enough for simple meals, considering she had a professional-sized one just a short walk away if she wanted to do anything more elaborate. There was no yard, but who needed a yard when she was just a few feet from the ocean? The beach would be her yard!

It was cheaper, too, than her place in LA, Ali thought as she paced into the bedroom for a second look. So once the lease ended on her old place, she'd technically be saving money. Well, assuming the bakery was able to turn a profit within the first month. Which might be easier said than done.

"This is just what I'm looking for," she said, coming back into the living room, where Teddy was so immersed in his character he was snootily inspecting the wiring.

Kerrigan looked thrilled. "I wish it was always this easy!" he exclaimed. He produced another contract from his suitcase, and another pen. "Déjà vu, eh?"

Ali took them both, perching on the edge of the couch. Now she'd found a place that could technically cost less than she was shelling out for before, she felt a lot less panicky about what she was doing. At least for now. It might be a different story when she was putting in twelve-

41

hour shifts seven days a week. But then again, Ali was used to waking up at the crack of dawn and slaving away in a hot kitchen while being scolded. At least this way, there wouldn't be anyone breathing down her neck, and her commute would be a stroll across the beach.

She signed on the dotted line and handed the contract back to Kerrigan.

He passed her the set of keys, thanked her, and left.

Ali shut the door behind him and turned to face Teddy. In unison, they began jumping up and down in the air, cheering. This was the celebration she should've had earlier if her panic hadn't set in.

"Teddy!" she squealed. "I can't believe this is happening!"

"I'm so happy for you!" he exclaimed, jumping around in circles with her.

"I need to phone my old landlord," Ali said, breathless. "Tell him I want to get out of my lease."

They stopped jumping, and Ali left Teddy in the living room to make the call in the privacy of the bedroom.

Her old landlord answered after a few rings and Ali briefly explained the situation with Otis.

"I need a fresh start," she said. "So I'm putting in my notice to leave."

"Great!" the landlord replied enthusiastically. "How long a notice period are you giving?"

Ali hadn't been expecting such excitement from him. "The two-month minimum."

"This is terrific news," he said. "I've been wanting to put the rent up for years but I'm not allowed until you go."

Ali was struck by a sudden inspiration. "I mean, I don't actually have to give any notice period, if you don't need me to. If you want the place back sooner, that works for me. I can be gone by ... well, the weekend."

Her landlord made a noise like he was choking on joy. "Really? Are you sure? You don't need more time to think about it?"

Ali looked around at the small bedroom that was soon to be hers and hers alone. She was more than ready to start her new life.

"I'm sure," she said, with finality. "This weekend will be my last."

CHAPTER NINE

Ali had thought it would be harder to leave LA. She'd lived there for three years, after all. She'd made a home for herself. At the very least she'd thought she would cry. But as she carried her last box down to her car, all she felt was relief.

She hadn't even noticed it happening, her life falling into a monotonous rut. But now she was suddenly free and she was thrilled to start her new dream.

The drive to Willow Bay felt way longer the second time around, because now Ali was desperate to get there, because she was so eager to start her new life. She felt like she was in a dream. Her life had done a complete 180.

She parked in the lot behind her row of cottages and began unloading her boxes, stacking them in the empty parking space. It was a Sahara-desert-hot day, and Ali was sweating from the drive. The ocean breeze on her brow was very welcome.

Ali's phone started to ring. She checked it and saw Hannah's name on the screen.

Hannah? What was Hannah doing calling her? Her sister never called.

Ali accepted the call, feeling worried. "What's wrong? Is it the kids? Jackson? Has something happened?"

"Everyone's fine," Hannah replied, in her usual flat affect. "It's you I'm worried about. Teddy said you're leaving LA?"

"I've already left," Ali said, looking at her stack of boxes.

"What happened?" Hannah pressed. "Teddy said you lost your job."

Ali put her hands on her hips. "What else did Teddy say?"

"Otis dumped you, you lost your job, and you're leaving LA," came Hannah's blunt reply.

Ali huffed. Was nothing sacred?

She shoved her cell between her ear and shoulder and lifted the first box into her arms.

"First of all, I didn't lose my job," she said, as she headed round the corner toward the front of the house. "I … instigated my departure from it."

"What the heck does that mean?" Hannah asked.

Ali reached her new front door. It was electric blue.

"It means I smooshed a crème brûlée with my fist all over a balding Hollywood exec," she said into her phone.

She placed the box down on the stoop. As she straightened up, she noticed the curtains of her new neighbor's house twitching, and a pair of eyes peeping suspiciously through the gap.

Ali waved brightly and the curtains flapped back into place.

With a shrug, Ali headed back around the corner to fetch the next box.

"That sounds like the actions of a totally sane person," Hannah said sarcastically in her ear. "And what's the deal with Otis? Teddy said he came out as gay."

Ali snatched up the next box. "Sounds like Teddy's already told you every last detail of my life."

"So it's true?" Hannah pressed. "Otis is gay?"

Ali twisted her lips to the side, a wave of melancholy washing over her. "Apparently so."

She began her next trip to her front door.

"Look, Allison," Hannah said. "I know it's probably very difficult to know you turned your boyfriend gay, but don't take it as a sign you need to change anything about yourself."

Ali stopped outside her front door and grimaced. "I didn't *turn* my boyfriend gay. It doesn't work like that."

The neighbor's curtains twitched again. Once again, Ali waved, and they snapped shut into place.

"I'm just saying don't get all insecure and think that you need to wear nicer clothes or get a better haircut," Hannah said bluntly. "You're fine the way you are."

"Gee," Ali said, dryly. "Thanks."

Of course Hannah was only trying to cheer her up, but she had a special brand of tactlessness that did nothing of the sort.

Ali headed to the lot for the final box.

"Hannah, why are you calling?" she asked.

"I wanted to see if you needed anything. Teddy said the place was a mess."

Ali rolled her eyes. She couldn't imagine Teddy talking about her behind her back (to Hannah of all people), but he was one to get a little bit carried away with a story, so she could see how her slightly scruffy store might be turned into a pigsty for drama's sake.

"I'll be fine, thanks," she said, lifting the last box. "I'm looking forward to doing the place up. I can decorate it just how I want."

She reached her door and unlocked it, then began relaying the boxes into the small, bare apartment.

"I'd better warn you that Mom knows about your little venture," Hannah said.

"She does?" Ali asked. "How did she find out already?"

Teddy hadn't blabbed to the both of them, had he? Ali was going to kill him!

"Your bank sent a letter," Hannah said. "They wanted to double-check the change of address wasn't fraudulent."

Ali frowned. Like most people, she'd bank-hopped over the years to get new customer deals, leaving a trail of breadcrumbs in her wake. But since she wasn't going to be able to just head home and pick up her mail whenever she felt like, she'd been careful to switch all her details. Something must have slipped through. Even so, any correspondence from the bank would be addressed to her, rather than her mother.

"Wasn't the letter addressed to me?"

"It was," Hannah said.

"But Mom still opened it?"

"Of course."

Ali rolled her eyes at the complete lack of privacy. Then she heard a beep in her ear that told her she had an incoming call.

"Hold on, Hannah. I'm getting another call." She checked the screen of her cell phone. It was their mom. "Speak of the devil."

"Is it her?" Hannah asked.

"Yeah. I'd better take it. You know how moody she gets when we don't answer her calls within five rings."

Hannah laughed. "Good luck," she said, before ending the call.

Ali connected to her mom's line.

"What took you so long to answer?" Georgia Sweet demanded.

"Hi, Mom, how are you? That's good. I'm fine, too thanks," Ali quipped.

Her mom sighed. "Yes, yes, very funny. So? Why did it take you so long to answer?"

"I was chatting with Hannah."

Ali knew her mom wouldn't stay mad if she knew the two sisters were talking. She was always worried about them not getting along well enough.

"That's nice," Georgia said. "Did she tell you how silly it is to be opening a store in this current economic climate?"

Ali's eyelids fluttered closed with mild frustration. "Actually she was just calling to wish me luck."

"Was she?" Georgia said, sounding surprised. "Because when we spoke yesterday she gave me a bunch of figures. Retail footfall is going down. Store rent is going up. People want to shop online these days, Ali. What makes you think you can run a store?"

"It's a bakery," Ali told her, firmly. "People don't buy pastries online, do they?"

"No. Because they don't buy them at all," Georgia said. "I mean, have you even done any market research? Hannah must've said a million times that the reason ninety percent of businesses fold in their first year is because they didn't realize there was little demand for what they were offering!"

Ali narrowed her eyes. Her mom's anxiety was practically oozing through the phone. It took all her patience to remind herself her mother was speaking from a place of love and concern, and not that she was just trying to dump on Ali's dreams.

Ali decided to try steering the conversation toward the positives.

"You should see it here, Mom," she said, walking to the window and peering out. "It's beautiful. I can see the ocean. There's a pier with rides on it. All the houses are painted colors of the rainbow..."

"It sounds like a hippie den. Why are you slumming it in a hippie den, Ali?"

"Mom! It's just a gorgeous, laidback seaside town."

But her mom wasn't listening. "What about your degree? And your doctorate? And your mentorship under Milo Baptiste? Doesn't any of that matter to you anymore? Are you really throwing that all away to make croissants?"

"Mom, all I was doing before was making crème brûlée. Now I'll be doing so much more. I'll be a business owner. A creator. I was basically a robot before. Now I'll actually get to use my brain."

"Using your brain means staying in a good job with decent health insurance, not going it alone. You're not thinking rationally."

Ali sighed. "You know what? You're right. I'm not thinking rationally. Because I thought rationally all my life and all that happened was I became a crème brûlée robot. So it's time to stop thinking rationally and start following my heart."

"Well," Georgia said, sounding affronted. "If that's how you feel, then so be it."

And with that, she hung up.

Ali stared at her phone, feeling like steam was billowing out of her ears. This was not how she'd wanted the first day of the rest of her life to begin.

With an angry huff, Ali knew what would make her feel better. Getting to work on her new store and paving the way to her future. She was going to prove her mother and her sister wrong.

CHAPTER TEN

A huge scraping noise came from behind Ali. She turned to the open door of her store, where Teddy was halfway through shoving a large stove inside. He'd driven down to help her set the store up, and the screech was quite obviously the sound of the stove damaging the floor.

"Teddy!" Ali exclaimed.

She hurried over to him. She'd chosen to wear denim overalls for their DIY day, and had tied her thick blond hair into two plaits with a fabric tie, because she may as well go the whole hog.

Teddy flashed her a guilty expression. "Sorry, sis."

She took one end of the stove, and together she and Teddy waddled it across the floor. As they went, an enormous dent was revealed in the peppermint green tiles.

"Perfect," Ali said. "That's my security deposit gone."

"Think of it as motivation," Teddy said. "Use it to fuel your ambition."

"That sounds like actor speak," she muttered.

They waddled the stove the rest of the way to the kitchen, which was currently in a state of complete disarray. Ali had happened across a big industrial sink from a nearby closing down restaurant and—getting a little too caught up in the serendipity of her new life—had lugged it back, decided to switch out the small one for it. Of course she didn't actually know how, and couldn't afford someone to do it for her, and so now there was just a big empty space filled with pipes.

"Do you need help with that?" Teddy asked, eyeing it warily. He was still puffing and panting from moving the stove.

Ali thought of the deep scratch on her floor and shook her head. "Nah. I think I've got this. Thanks anyway."

Teddy flopped forward onto the counter. "Thank god. I'm exhausted. I couldn't lift another thing."

He closed his eyes, clearly already giving up on his offer to help her fix up the place.

Ali looked at the sink.

I guess it's just you and me, she thought.

*

Ali wielded a wrench and hit play on the internet tutorial entitled "How to Install a Sink: The Plumber's Step-by-Step Guide."

She'd sent Teddy home. He was becoming more of an encumbrance to her DIY day than a help, so she decided to get the work done alone.

She watched the tutorial and tried her best to follow along with the instructions. It was like listening to a foreign language. Pipes this, caulks that, clamps, connectors, and brackets. Ali flapped about, trying her best to keep track of all the steps as she went.

When she was done, she stepped back and admired her handiwork. The industrial-sized sink looked just perfect. Ali felt rather satisfied with herself.

She tried the faucet and a stream of water flowed out.

Ali punched the air. "HAHA!" she exclaimed, dancing on the spot from foot to foot.

Then she frowned. Steam? Why was there steam coming out of the faucet?

Ali realized that hot water was coming out of the cold tap. She quickly shut it off and tried the hot tap. Ice cold.

"Of course," she muttered aloud to herself. She'd installed it the wrong way around. "Rookie mistake."

Just then, she heard footsteps and turned to see a suave-looking Italian man entering the store. It was the man from the pizzeria she and Teddy had eaten at on their first trip here. He was holding a wicker basket that appeared to be stuffed with goodies. A welcome basket!

Ali grinned as the man approached the counter, and wiped the grease from the wrench onto her overalls—something she'd seen the sassy heroine in movies do and had always wanted to emulate.

"Marco, isn't it?" she asked warmly.

In a split second, the man's smile dropped. "It's Emilio," he corrected.

"Emilio?" Ali repeated, confused. "But I was in your pizzeria the other day. You served me a margherita pizza."

"I did nothing of the sort," the man said, brusquely. "You must've gone to Marco's pizzeria. He's my brother."

Ali's mouth dropped open. "Wait... Are you twins?"

49

"Unfortunately," he said with a grimace. "But Marco's pizzas are overpriced and his ingredients are poor quality."

Ali smirked, recalling that Marco had said the same about Emilio's pizzas when she'd eaten there.

So the bitter rivals on either side of her were *twins*. And she was going to be right in the middle of two bickering brothers. Two attractive Italian brothers. This was going to be a hoot and a half...

"Anyway, enough about *him*," Emilio said in a strong, swoon-inducing accent. "I wanted to bring you a moving in gift." He placed the basket on the counter. It was full of different-shaped pastas.

"How kind of you," Ali said.

"It's nice to have someone in this store again," Emilio continued. "Pete was a nice man. Popular. I was very fond of him."

Fond of him, or fond of the buffer? Ali wondered.

Before Ali had a chance to ask more about Pete, a dog came trotting in through the open door. It was a brown and black terrier, semi-longhaired. It came up to Emilio's shins and halted next to him.

"Your dog is so cute!" Ali squealed. She loved dogs almost as much as she loved cats.

Emilio looked down at the terrier. "Him? No. He's a stray. Lives on the boardwalk. He's always sniffing around for scraps. We call him Scruff."

"Scruff!" Ali exclaimed. It was too cute for words.

She went around the counter, crouched down, and petted him. He gazed at her with his big brown eyes. Ali's heart melted.

"He'll never leave you alone now," Emilio said from above.

Ali looked up at him. "That's fine by me."

She'd always dreamed of owning a dog. She couldn't really have one in her small apartment, so maybe having a doggy visitor stop by her store on occasion would satisfy that urge.

"Hello!" a voice called.

Emilio visibly bristled. "See you," he said, before hurrying past the new intruder.

It was a woman, hippie-ish, with soft white-blond hair hanging all the way down her back. She was slim and muscular, and dripping with jewelry.

"Bye, Emilio!" she trilled as the Italian man hurried away. Then she looked at Ali and grinned. "Hello, neighbor!"

"Hi," Ali said, feeling intimidated by the ebullient beauty standing in front of her. Typical that they'd meet when Ali was dressed in dirty overalls.

"I'm Delaney," the woman continued. "I work up the road. My store is called Little Bits of This and That." She thrust a flyer at Ali. "Thought I'd come in and say hello. See how you're settling in." She spoke very quickly, and her gaze darted all over the place like a hawk.

"Thanks," Ali said, a little taken aback. "I'm Ali."

"What's your plan with this place?" Delaney asked.

"Pastries," Ali said. "I'm a pâtissier."

"Oh, how novel," Delany said. "I simply adore French cuisine. And it's not the sort of thing you'd find on the boardwalk, so that's lovely and unique."

Ali was wary. She couldn't tell if that was a backhanded compliment or not.

"Do you know what happened to Pete?" Delaney asked.

Ali shrugged. "No idea."

"It's a shame," Delaney replied. "He made the best pitas. Honestly. Such a lovely man. I hope he's okay. He didn't have much business acumen. Not to toot my own horn, but there's an art to this and some people just don't have it." She laughed loudly. "Anyway, I just wanted to pop in and say hi, and say I look forward to getting to know you— and take my advice." She lowered her voice. "Don't date either of the Italians." Then she brightened again. "Toodles!" she said, and off she went.

Ali watched her go, feeling like a hurricane had just swept through her store.

*

At the end of a long day of DIY, Ali decided to sit on the beach to watch the sunset. She'd been working hard renovating the store, and deserved a bit of time to soak it all in.

The beach was pretty quiet, with just a few dog walkers and joggers, and a solitary man out surfing in the waves. Ali watched his silhouette as she munched on the ham and pickle sandwich she'd made for dinner.

The surfer started doing tricks in the waves. Ali watched, impressed. But suddenly he mistimed a wave and his board smacked him in the face.

"Oh no!" Ali cried, jumping up and running for the water.

The man bobbed back up. Blood was running from his nose. He spotted her running for him.

"I'm all right," he called, in a distinctly Australian accent.

"You're bleeding!" Ali called back, kicking up surf as she ran.

He touched his nose, then inspected his fingers covered in blood.

"You're right," he said. "Flippin' hell!"

Ali reached him, her overalls now soaked up to the thighs, and shoved the napkin from her sandwich at him.

"Take this," she said.

"Thanks," he said, dabbing his nose.

He wasn't much taller than Ali. Up close, she could see he was handsome, in an unsuspecting way. He had a boyishness to his features, with round cheeks, freckles, and a turned up nose. His hair was dark blond, but naturally highlighted by the combination of sea and sunshine, as surfers' hair often was. It was slightly too long, sticking in tendrils to his tanned face. He was in many ways the opposite of Ali's usual type—tall, dark (and gay, apparently)—but Ali found herself somewhat inexplicably attracted to him. Maybe it was the fact he was in distress and she was there to rescue him. Or maybe it was the way water was dripping down his golden skin and through the defined muscles on his torso like rivulets. Whatever it was, her stomach was doing back flips.

"I hate the sight of blood," he said in that strong Aussie accent. "Makes me woozy."

"I'll help you," Ali offered, jumping at the chance.

She took him by the elbow and steered him to the shore. Once they were on the sand, he flopped down and let his board fall beside him.

"You must think I'm a right wuss," he said, his voice distorted by the tissue he had wadded beneath his nose.

Ali sat on the sand beside him, keeping at least an arm's-length distance between them, since she was so tempted to reach out and touch his muscles. "If you're brave enough to surf, you can't be a wuss," she said.

"Brave? Nah. The waves out here are piddly. I've had much worse accidents happen out on Bondi."

"Bondi Beach?" Ali asked, dreamily, imaging this handsome man cutting the waves on one of the world's best beaches. "I figured you're Australian."

He propped himself up on his elbows, the bloodied tissue sticking out of his nostrils.

"What gave it away?" he joked.

Ali couldn't help but laugh at the sight of him, and his funny demeanor. He put her at ease. "I think that's going to bruise," she said, peering at his injury.

He gave a laid-back shrug. "Ah well. I'm collecting battle scars."

Ali felt herself relaxing into his company.

"So, what are you doing in Willow Bay?" she asked. "Because you're obviously not here for the piddly waves."

"I live here," he said. "I own a store here."

"Really?" Ali asked, surprised they had something in common. "Which one?"

"Whitewater," he said, pointing down the boardwalk. "The surf shop."

Ali blushed. Obviously he owned the surf shop. You didn't get a body like that selling donuts.

"There's nothing like ending a shift at the store and going for a surf," he said, smiling into the distance. "The ocean's my playground. It's heaven."

"Hmmm," Ali murmured dreamily.

"Oh, I'm Nate, by the way," he said, offering his spare, non-blood-soaked hand.

"Ali," she said, taking it. "I just opened a store here."

"You did?" He sounded suddenly enthused.

"Yup. It used to be Pete's Pitas."

"Pete's closed?" Nate asked, sounding distraught. "Damn. Those pitas were something."

"So I've been told," Ali said. She was starting to get nervous about the clearly big shoes she was trying to fill.

"Any idea what happened?" Nate asked. "Pete's was super popular."

Ali shrugged. "Sorry, I don't know."

"Maybe he made so much money he retired early," Nate said. "Who knows—maybe you'll be next!"

"I doubt that," Ali said, chuckling.

"So what are you going to use the store for?" Nate asked.

"Pastries," Ali said. "I'm a pâtissier."

"Sounds fancy."

The sun was beginning to descend, taking with it most of the warmth of the evening.

"I'd better get home," Nate said.

He stood and held his hand out for her to help her up. Ali took it, feeling a blush creep into her cheeks.

"It was nice to meet you," she said, bashfully. "Maybe I'll bump into you again some time. It's a pretty small town, after all."

Nate wiggled his brows. "I hope so."

Ali's heart double-kicked.

That was flirting, right? He was definitely flirting?

Feeling incredibly flustered, Ali gave him a wave and stepped back. But Nate took a step forward.

"Looks like we're going the same direction," he said with a smirk.

"Where do you live?" Ali asked as they paced side by side along the beach in the direction of the colorful cottages.

"House with the green door," he said, pointing to the row of shoreside apartments on the very same alleyway as Ali's new place was. In fact, she realized when they arrived there, he was just a few doors down from her.

"In which case we definitely will be seeing each other again," Ali said, feeling her lips tug up into a smile.

"I look forward to it," Nate told her.

Then he headed in through his own front door.

Ali felt her cheeks flush with warmth. She hurried inside her apartment, shut the door, and pressed her back against it, feeling giddy.

Delaney had said not to date either of the Italians. But she hadn't said a word about Australians…

CHAPTER ELEVEN

"Voilà!" Ali said, gently placing a caramel tart into the fridge to complete the display.

It was opening day. Ali had baked and DIY'd her way here, and now had a great range of gourmet pastries, cakes, and desserts to offer to the good people of Willow Bay. There was just one last thing left to do. Find a name.

Delaney was sitting in the window seat—upholstered by Ali's own fair hand using a selection of old curtains from the local thrift store and an industrial-sized stapler. Her knee was crooked up, showing off an anklet around her tanned ankle, and her white-blond hair was swept over one shoulder. On the cushions by her sandaled feet was Ali's notepad of name ideas, which she was scanning with squinched eyes.

She'd offered to paint a sign for Ali on a bit of driftwood she'd found on the beach. Ali had jumped at the offer, since she'd just about reached the end of her patience when it came to painting, and Delaney had significantly more artistic talent than herself.

"I'm adding *Coastal Confections*," Delaney said as she glanced down the list in Ali's notebook of ideas. "I am convinced alliteration is the way to go."

She added her idea in cursive handwriting that was as pretty and floaty as she was herself.

Ali came and sat opposite her.

"It's a bit fussy, isn't it?" she said.

"Fittingly so," Delaney said, gesturing to the display fridge filled with banoffee pies, profiteroles, peach pavlovas and palmiers. "I can't even pronounce half the things you make."

Ali laughed. "I get where you're coming from, but I don't want my store to have an arrogant vibe. I don't want it to seem exclusive. I may be selling fancy desserts, but I want them to be for everyone."

"Well, what vibe do you want?" Delaney asked.

Ali looked around. She'd collected a whole bunch of dining tables, proper 1950s ones from an old ice cream parlor. Then she'd upholstered all the chairs with pale blue gingham to match the peppermint floor. The blinds were white. The shelves were pastel green.

"Kitsch?" Ali suggested.

"Kitsch Kitchen," Delaney offered.

Ali shook her head.

"Dainty Desserts?"

Ali stuck out her tongue.

"Yummy Scrummy?"

Ali just laughed. This shouldn't be so hard. But it was important. She didn't want to rush it just because she was supposed to be opening her doors today. This name would stick with her forever. Or at least as long as she was able to keep her business afloat. She needed a name that would become part of the fabric of Willow Bay, much like Pete's Pitas clearly had. It had to be simple, but personal and friendly at the same time.

"How about just Sweet's?" Ali said, printing the name in the air with her hands. "It would be a crime not to use my last name."

"I like it," Delaney said. "It's cute. But it feels like it's missing something." She gazed out the window. "Beach Sweets."

"Seaside Sweets!" Ali exclaimed.

Delaney looked back at her, her eyes wide like the muse had struck. "That's it! That's the one! I'm on it!" She grabbed a tube of paint and squeezed out a glob.

"Seaside Sweets," Ali said again, trying it out for size. She liked it.

She grabbed her phone and quickly texted Teddy. He'd been on tenterhooks to find out what she finally decided to name the place.

Are you ready? Seaside Sweets is about to open its doors!

A few seconds later, Teddy's reply buzzed onto her phone. *I love it! Now, don't forget those pearls!*

Ali laughed, remembering how she'd told Teddy how she wanted to work in a bakery and wear pearls like Julia Child.

If only, Ali replied.

Check your mail, woman! came Teddy's response.

Ali frowned. In all the chaos of getting the store ready she hadn't even thought about such a boring and practical matter as actually checking her mail. She glanced over the pile she'd accumulated and saw, almost immediately, the one that did not belong amongst all the plain white company letters and fast food flyers: a bulging, bright pink envelope.

Ali unfolded her legs from beneath her and hurried over. As soon as she'd snatched it up, she recognized Teddy's terrible handwriting. He'd addressed it to *Princess Allison the Sweet.*

Ali chuckled and ripped open the top. A cute faux pearl necklace fell from it.

Touched, Ali scooped it up. A note fluttered to the ground beside it. She picked it up and began to read.

Now before you say anything about how much this cost, Hannah also chipped in. Congrats for making your dreams come true.

Ali was so touched. Of course he was joking about the cost—the pearls were clearly fake ones that wouldn't cost that much at all—but it only made her love the gift even more. She wiped away a tear from her eye.

"You okay, hon?" Delaney asked from her window seat.

Ali swirled. "I'm good. I'm great." She put the necklace on. "I'm ready to open those doors!"

She hurried over to the glass door. Delaney joined her at her side.

"Are you wearing pearls?" she asked.

"It's a family joke," Ali told her.

Then she unlocked the door and threw it wide open.

Ali had pictured this moment a hundred times since moving to Willow Bay. In her daydreams, the hordes of tourists and locals came flooding in and cleared her shelves immediately. Of course that didn't happen in reality. Instead, a solitary seagull looked at her and blinked, before taking flight.

She let her arms drop. "I guess it'll take a little while for people to realize I'm open."

She gazed left and right, from Marco's seating area to Emilio's. Every single one of their tables was occupied. There were plenty of people milling along the boardwalk, too. But no one gave her store even a cursory glance.

"It'll get better once the sign's up," Delaney offered.

She went back to the window seat to continue painting it.

Ali hoped she was right. At the moment, all there was, was a sad chalkboard she'd drawn for the occasion.

Suddenly, she noticed a woman marching purposefully toward her store, and her heart leapt.

"Someone's coming," she squealed.

Delaney was too absorbed in her task to even look up, with her tongue poking from the side of her mouth in concentration. All she did was grunt an acknowledgment.

Ali hurried behind the counter, ready to greet her first ever customer.

The woman entered.

"Welcome to Seaside Sweets!" Ali exclaimed, grinning from ear to ear. "How can I help you today?"

"Help me, darling?" the woman purred. "Why, you've already done plenty by opening up."

Ali frowned, confused.

Delaney's head snapped up as if the voice was familiar to her.

"Miriyam," she said.

The woman looked over her shoulder. "Oh, Delaney. Hello. I didn't notice you there."

She had a pompous tone, Ali noted, and by the look of trepidation in Delaney's eyes, she guessed she wasn't a welcome visitor after all.

The woman peered back at Ali. "I'm Miriyam. I own another bakery on the boardwalk. I must say, it's good to have another upscale store. All these surf shops and pizza joints really bring down the pizzazz. Willow Bay used to be more upscale. It's been sliding recently. So I'm pleased to see you here." She peered at the fridge and all the goodies being offered. "Yes. This will do nicely. Your prices are a little on the low side though. Perhaps jack them up a little. You won't turn much profit otherwise. Stores of our caliber don't get much footfall."

Behind her, Delaney made a face. Ali smirked. Miriyam snapped her head over her shoulder suspiciously.

"Seaside Sweets?" she said, reading the sign Delaney had skillfully sketched onto the driftwood. "Oh no. That's a terrible name. It sounds far too informal. You need something much more grand than that."

"My surname is Sweet," Ali said. "Get it? It's a play on words. Kind of."

Miriyam did not look impressed. Ali's smile slid off her face.

"What's your store called?" she asked, attempting to overcome the awkwardness.

"Cookies," Miriyam replied.

"Cookies?" Ali echoed. "I don't think I've noticed it yet. Where did you say you were located?"

"Other side of the boardwalk," Miriyam said brusquely. "You must have seen me."

Ali snapped her fingers. "I remember now. It's Kookies with a K, right?"

Miriyam pursed her lips and narrowed her eyes. "What do you mean with a K? How else would it be spelled?"

"With a C," Ali said, simply. "Cookie is spelled with a C."

She noticed too late Delaney's desperate hand gestures and attempts to get her to abort her sentence. Miriyam's face turned thunderous. Ali felt her features drop.

"Goodbye, Miss Sweet," Miriyam said, huffing out.

Ali got the distinct impression she'd made her first enemy.

CHAPTER TWELVE

Ali straightened up the croissants for what felt like the hundredth time that day. But it wasn't like there was anything else to do. All day, her store had been almost completely empty.

Just then, a woman came in holding hands with a small kid. Ali's heart skipped. Kids loved dessert.

"I need to use your bathroom," the mom announced dramatically. "This one drank a whole liter of pop."

Ali looked down at the tubby little boy clutching her hand. His brown hair was messy from swimming in the ocean.

"What did I tell you about fizzy drinks?" she said gruffly.

Ali sunk her head onto her fist. Of course the woman wasn't here to buy anything. No one else had all day. A few people had come in to check out the refurb, or to ask what happened to Pete's Pitas, but Ali had made precisely zero sales.

"Through there," she said, glumly, jabbing her thumb over her shoulder in the direction of the bathroom, wondering why the kid hadn't just peed in the sea like any other five-year-old would do.

The woman tugged the kid's hand. But the kid did not move. He dug his heels in.

The mom frowned.

With sudden dawning horror, Ali realized what had happened. The child had already peed, all over her peppermint-tiled floor.

"Duncan!" his mom yelled. "What have I told you?"

Duncan promptly burst into tears. Because of course the only thing that would make the fact there was pee all over her floor worse was the high-pitched shrill wailing of a child.

With a sigh, Ali left the counter and headed for the cleaning supplies closet at the back of the kitchen. At least it gave her an opportunity to use the cute floral print mop and bucket she'd brought online.

She retrieved them from the cupboard and headed out through the side door into the seating area of the store. Poor Duncan was still getting an earful from his angry mother.

"You got it all over your shoes!" she was screeching. "I'm going to have to put them in the washing machine when we get home, and tonight I was planning to wash whites!"

Ali flashed him a pitying smile. As annoying as it was that he'd made a disgusting mess on her floor, she still didn't like watching his mom berate him like that.

At the sight of Ali's kind face, Duncan stopped crying. He blinked at her, looking confused that an adult was showing him an ounce of kindness. Then his perplexed expression disappeared, and in a split second he stuck his finger right in the middle of one of the sweet-glazed French crullers, pulled out a sticky finger covered in cream, and shoved it right in his mouth. He grinned in a way Ali could only describe as devilish.

"Hey!" she exclaimed.

But Duncan was being frog-marched away by his ranting mom, who seemed to have completely forgotten Ali was there, or that she owed her an apology for the havoc she'd caused.

Ali gritted her teeth. She grabbed the spoiled French cruller and threw it in the bin. Then she got to work mopping up Duncan's puddle of urine.

This day had been a terrible disaster. She'd offended Miriyam. She hadn't sold a thing. And now she was mopping up pee.

She heard a noise and looked up, anticipating the next disaster. A seagull was standing in her open doorway, with beady, questioning eyes.

"Hey, buddy," she said, wondering if making conversation with a seagull was the first sign of madness. "Can I help you?"

He squawked, his yellow bill opening and closing again, as if in response to her question.

Ali couldn't help herself. She giggled. A friendly seagull might just be the antidote she needed to her sad and stressful day.

"What was that?" Ali asked, immediately going into improv mode. "You said you'd like to purchase a sweet-glazed French cruller, preferably one that a little boy has stuck his finger into? Well, you're just in luck. I have one right here in the trash can. Freshly poked. And you, sir, can have it for free."

She rested the mop against the wall and leaned into the trash to retrieve it, only to hear the sudden sound of flapping wings behind her. She turned sharply to discover the seagull had flown inside her store and snatched up a croissant! It flapped away, cackling as it went.

"Thief!" Ali cried, waving her fist the bird.

She slammed the door shut.

Great. So she wouldn't be able to leave that open now. Which meant she'd probably have to shell out for proper air conditioning. Her simple desk fan wasn't going to cut it.

She felt deflated. What else could possibly go wrong?

Just then, the door flew open and a man stormed inside. He had dark greasy hair hanging in limp tendrils over his dark beady eyes. His round tummy protruded over the waistband of his ill-fitting pants. He didn't look like your average Californian, to say the least.

He stopped right in the middle of the store, glancing around with a thoroughly unimpressed look on his face.

Ali gulped. She had a very bad feeling about this.

"Can I help you?" Ali asked, tentatively.

The man's black eyes snapped to her.

"Who the hell are you?" he said gruffly.

Ali felt herself shrinking back under his stare. She wondered whether he was a crazed Pete's Pitas fan come to demand she leave town and give him back his beloved pita place.

"I'm Ali," she said, forcing a strained smile onto her face. "Welcome to Seaside Sweets."

"Seaside Sweets?" he repeated, bitterly, almost spitting out the word with distaste. "I've never heard such a dreadful name. And what do we need another sweet shop for anyway? We have Kookies!"

Ali felt herself withering from the force of his fury. Peeing kids and croissant-stealing seagulls she could cope with. But angry, rude men getting right in her face? She'd had enough of that during her Éclairs days to ever want to experience it again.

Ali suddenly became acutely aware of just how alone she was in the store. At least in Éclairs there'd been people around to stop things getting out of hand. But here, it was just her and a furious-looking man, squaring off. He had a good few inches on her, and plenty of body mass.

Ali puffed herself up. "If you're not here to buy anything, then I think you should leave," she said, trying her best to be bold.

"Leave?" he sneered. "Me? If anyone should leave, it's you! You're the thief!"

His words surprised her. Ali frowned, perplexed.

"Excuse me?" she asked, affronted by the bizarre accusation.

62

"This store was supposed to be mine," the man said. "Mine!" Then he stamped his foot, like an actual child throwing a tantrum, and pointed his finger at the floor. "Kerrigan promised it to me."

At the mention of her landlord, Ali's mind swirled. There seemed to be more to this man's accusations than she'd expected. Perhaps they weren't the baseless rantings of a madman.

"Kerrigan O'Neal?" Ali asked, surprised.

"Of course Kerrigan O'Neal!" the man cried. "How many Kerrigan O'Neals do you think there are in Willow Bay! Are you an imbecile as well as a thief!"

Ali's heart was starting to race. She did not like this altercation one bit, and she was afraid where it might go.

"I—I'm sorry. I didn't know. Did you have a contract with Kerrigan?"

"We had a verbal agreement," the man snapped. "Next thing I know, you're here!"

He sneered, like Ali was a bad smell.

Ali felt terrible. It was never her intention to undercut someone. No wonder the man was so furious—though he should be taking it out on her landlord really, not her. She was an innocent victim, caught in the middle of something she'd never intended.

"I'm so sorry if I stepped on your toes..." she began.

But the man cut her off. "IF?" he yelled. "IF? Oh, there's no if about it. You did! You snatched this place right out from underneath me!"

Ali held her hands up in a truce. It seemed that no matter what she said, the man got more and more angry. She had no idea how to bring a peaceful resolution to this terrible altercation.

"I really had no idea," she said.

"A likely story!" the man cried with indignation. "I bet you offered him a sweet deal, didn't you? What was it? Did you offer over the asking price? And pay for the renovations yourself?"

She had paid for the renovations herself, but only after Teddy's shrewd negotiation skills had secured her the first month rent for free.

"Honestly, I didn't mean to undercut anyone," Ali said. "If I did, I'm truly sorry."

"I don't buy that for one second," the man shouted. He marched to the door, throwing it wide open so all and sundry could hear the commotion. "Mark my words, miss. I'll ruin this place!"

63

He marched out, bellowing, "Don't shop here, people! This place is run by a criminal!"

Ali watched him go, flabbergasted, her cheeks burning with embarrassment. Of all the awful things to go wrong today, that really had been the worst.

She braced herself. If all that could happen on day one, what else could go wrong for her?

CHAPTER THIRTEEN

Ali swiped all her unsold pastries into a big plastic bag, then headed out the door of her store into the warm California evening.

A horrible sense of dread weighed on her chest. Not only had her grand opening been a disappointing disaster, actually losing her money, but the altercation with the man had left her rattled. If any of his accusations had a semblance of truth, she'd become the town pariah in days. She was tempted to march up to Kerrigan O'Neal and give him a piece of her mind. But she was too close to tears to even risk it. It wouldn't do much for her carefully constructed famous-pastry-chef persona to turn up on his doorstep blubbering about the mean man who'd called her a thief.

She turned to lock the door behind her, disappointment setting in.

"Ali, hey," a male voice said.

She swirled. It was Nate, looking exceptionally handsome in the moonlight and glow of store lights.

"Nate," Ali said, surprised. "What are you doing here?"

"I came to see how your grand opening went," he said. He grinned his pearly-toothed grin and flashed her an expectant look.

Ali shifted self-consciously from foot to foot. "Em..."

"Uh-oh," Nate said, softly. "What happened?"

His jokey exterior vanished, and he was now looking at her with kindness. Ali was a little taken aback by his perceptiveness. Otis could never tell she was sad unless tears were literally streaming down her cheeks. It was refreshing.

"It was a total bust," Ali told him, unable to keep the glumness from her voice.

He winced with sympathy. "How bad?"

"Really, really bad." Ali shook her head as she spoke. "Like, no customers bad. Like a kid peed on my floor bad. Like a seagull shoplifted me bad." She couldn't help but let out a sad, wry laugh.

"I'm sorry, Ali," Nate said, gently. "That sucks. But try not to take it personally. You're brand new. People will need a little bit of time to warm up to you."

She scuffed the toe of her shoe against the other. "I guess. How long did it take you to get customers?"

"I mean, I'm a surf shop," Nate said, sounding like he was trying to be tactful, "so, like, we totally have a different customer base. But…"

"It was right away, wasn't it?" Ali guessed. "You were a hit from day one?"

Nate shrugged. "Kinda."

Ali sighed. As much as she appreciated his attempts to cheer her up, he'd actually inadvertently solidified what she already knew: she was a terrible businesswoman.

"I'd better get home," she said. "This bag of unsold pastries isn't going to eat itself."

"You're eating that whole bag?" Nate said, eyes widening. "You're not even going to share them with me? Down on the beach?" He gave her a friendly nudge.

Despite her sadness, Ali was able to rouse a smile.

"All right," she said.

What else was she going to do? Go home alone and cry into her bag of unsold pastries? Might as well spend her moping time with a handsome Australian surfer.

She held her bag out to him. "Pick your poison."

He reached inside. "It's like a lucky dip," he said, plucking out a cannelé. "What's this little guy?" he asked.

Ali giggled. "It's a cannelé. It's like a little pastry parcel of vanilla and caramel." She remembered learning all about them with Milo Baptiste. He'd actually insisted they go to Bordeaux, the town they originated from, to make sure she learned how to make it authentically.

Nate popped it in his mouth in one go. His eyes widened as he chewed. "That's incredible!"

"Thanks," Ali said, shyly. "Want another?"

Nate eagerly stuck his hand back in the bag. This time he pulled out a croissant. "Classic," he said, smiling brightly.

They headed down to the beach together. The water was gentle, the waves breaking rhythmically and softly against the shore. They strolled close to the shoreline where the sand was wet, leaving a trail of footprints behind them.

"Did you say you got shoplifted by a seagull?" Nate asked.

Ali tipped her head back and barked out a laugh. "Yeah. While I was in the middle of mopping up pee."

"Dude," Nate said. "That sucks." He took a bite of his croissant. "Whoa! Ali! This is amazing!"

"Thanks," Ali said. "Too bad no one around here wants to buy one."

"You know," Nate said mid-chew, "Whitewater might've had customers, but most people who came through the doors were teenagers with big dreams, tons of questions, and hardly any cash. I didn't turn a profit for years."

"Really?" Ali asked.

"Yup. It's a hard slog. It's not going to come overnight. But here's some advice. You need to win over the locals first. All those poor teens who came in asking me surfing questions in the first months... well, guess what they got their parents to buy them for Christmas? Surfboards."

"I don't think many teenagers have a passion for pastry," Ali said.

"Not teenagers," Nate said. "But what about middle-aged ladies? Do you know how many stay-at-home moms there are in Willow Bay? How many retirees? I see them all power-walking in the mornings. You know, if you get up at the crack of dawn, maybe you can catch them. Ingratiate yourself into their ranks. Infiltrate. I take it you have neon sweats."

Ali smirked. "I get up at dawn to bake, anyway. It's the only way to get the pastries ready in time for the breakfast crowd."

If there's ever going to be a breakfast crowd, Ali thought ruefully.

It was sweet of Nate to try and cheer her up, but it wasn't going to work. A group of power-walking fifty-somethings was hardly going to make the difference.

"There was another bad thing that happened today," Ali said. "Apparently someone else was promised the lease of the store, until I accidentally undercut him. I didn't even realize I was doing that. My landlord seemed desperate to get it off his hands. I assumed no one else had shown any interest."

"Ali," Nate said, firmly but kindly. "This is business. Things like that happen all the time. Whoever this guy was, it sounds like he took it personally. And it sounds like you did too. Let it go. What does it matter? You'll tread on more people's toes over time. As long as you're not malevolent and ruthless about it, then you shouldn't feel guilty."

Ali regarded him. "Thanks," she said.

Maybe Nate's sweetness did work. She actually did feel a bit better about the whole thing.

67

They reached the end of the pier. It was still in full swing, its lights blazing, its music blaring.

"Nate, I think I'm going to take a walk along the pier, if that's cool with you," Ali said. "On my own."

"You sure?" he asked.

Ali nodded. "I'm feeling better."

"Good." Then he smiled cheekily. "Can I get another croissant for the road?"

"Of course!" Ali exclaimed, glad that at least someone in this town liked her pastries. "Take a couple for breakfast as well."

"Awesome." He pulled three more from her bag and waved them at her as he walked backward. "Thanks, Ali. See you tomorrow. And chin up, yeah?"

Ali smiled as he turned and walked away with a little bounce in his step.

Ali headed through the entrance to the pier, walking slowly so she could breathe in the sea air of her new home. It had been a bad day, but Nate's advice and words of wisdom had cheered her.

She reached the end of the pier and looked up at the moon. She was suddenly hit by a pang of nostalgia for her dad. She thought she'd put all those feelings to bed many years ago, but now, being back here, they'd resurfaced. It turned out she missed him after all.

She wondered what he'd say if he could see her now.

And with that thought, Ali realized she couldn't ever give up. She had to do whatever it took to make her bakery a success.

*

Once Ali had baked the next morning's haul of pastries, she decided to take Nate's advice about the power walkers. Feeling optimistic, she filled a bag with still-warm pastries, locked up the store, and headed out with a renewed spring in her step.

It had turned into a fresh, brisk morning. Ali headed down to the sandy beach, glancing about until she caught a glimpse of the neon-clad power walkers in the distance, advancing across the sand like a stampede of lurid colored buffalo.

I should've stretched, she thought. *Those women are fast!*

The space between them closed, and Ali readied herself to join their march. Then suddenly, they were beside her and she took off alongside them.

"Hi!" she exclaimed, marching in time. "I'm Ali."

A gray-haired woman with a pink sweatband looked at her and smiled.

"Morning!" she said without missing a beat. "I'm Irene."

Ali decided not to offer her hand to shake. The woman was using both arms to help propel her brisk march. Ali had to hop-skip just to keep up with her.

"I just opened a bakery," Ali explained. She was already short of breath. "Would you like to try one of my pastries?"

She offered the bag.

"No thanks, darling," Irene said. "I don't do carbs."

Ali was about to move on to the next power walker, but a sudden scream pierced the tranquil morning. The seagulls took to the sky in a flurry. The scream was so guttural, Ali felt it right in her bones.

"What was that?" she gasped.

Her heart began to race.

Then the first scream was joined by another, though it sounded like it was from a different person.

Uneasy, Ali scanned the beach. She noticed a small crowd had formed on the shoreline, over near the pier. Even from this distance she could see their distress.

She and the power walkers hurried over to see what was going on.

There was something large and dark lying in the surf, tangled in a net, next to a very distraught-looking fisherman. At first Ali thought it was a seal. But then she realized it was too big for that.

"I—I snagged him on the line," the fisherman stammered. "I pulled him in."

Him? Ali thought.

She took a step closer to the dark lump on the coast. It was human. It was a body. A man.

Ali suddenly gasped as she realized she recognized him. It was the guy who'd accused her of being a thief yesterday!

Now here he was, dead in the water.

CHAPTER FOURTEEN

Ali watched with apprehension as the police arrived in a convoy of flashing lights—two regular cop cars and one black Mercedes with tinted windows. From the more intimidating vehicle, two detectives emerged—a statuesque woman who appeared to be the one in charge, and her shorter, preppy-looking male partner, whose appearance was more health inspector than murder detective.

Ali watched them approach with equal parts nerves and fascination.

"Everyone back!" the woman commanded.

Ali huddled with the other neon-clad power walkers, feeling like sheep being herded into a pen. The detectives got to work orchestrating the scene with the efficiency of stagehands on opening night. Except, of course, this was no play. There really was a dead body lying beneath that white sheet.

Ali struggled to take it all in. Her day had started so optimistically, but it had veered dramatically off course, sending her in a new direction she was barely able to comprehend. She shuddered as she thought of the dead man on the sand, the man who'd shouted at her and insulted her just half a day earlier. She became acutely aware that his death would be a part of her forever.

"Do you think it was suicide?" a voice whispered in her ear.

Ali flinched. Irene, the pink-sweatband-wearing, carb-avoiding power walker, had crept up beside her, close enough for her breath to tickle Ali's earlobe. Ali wasn't the sort of person to get her kicks out of gossiping about someone else's misfortune, particularly in circumstances so gruesome and grizzly.

"I hope not," she replied, her gaze fixed on the long white lump in the sand.

If the man had killed himself, could it have been over his lost store? It didn't bear thinking about. That would make her complicit, in a sense. She'd have to live with that guilt forever.

"What about murder?" Irene whispered.

Ali frowned at her. Irene's gray eyes were sparkling with glee and Ali found it rather distasteful. This was a real dead human being they were talking about, not some throwaway character in a cop procedural. Whether the victim had died by his own hand, another's, or some terrible freak accident was incidental. It was a tragedy. All Ali could think of was the human life that had been snuffed out before its time, and all the friends and family left behind to cope. She knew a little bit herself about what it felt like to try and make sense of life when one of your loved ones was suddenly no longer in it.

Thankfully, the sound of heavy vehicles approaching put an end to Irene's scandal-mongering.

Ali glanced over to see two white vans crawling down the sand toward the shore. Their presence was surreal; they looked so out of place, like two shiny white snails leaving tire trails in the sand behind them. On one van, the letters CSI were printed, dark blue against the lurid white. On the other, K-9. Ali knew from TV that meant the first was transporting the crime scene investigators and their equipment, the second the canine units. As an animal lover, Ali had no control over her sudden surge of excitement at seeing the sniffer dogs, but then she reminded herself just how inappropriate that would be in this context, and tempered her enthusiasm.

Ali tightened her arms about her middle, suddenly feeling cold as she watched the beach transform from a place of lazy tranquility into a busy, high-octane crime scene. Everything seemed to be happening at once. A dozen or so CSIs hopped down from the van, swiftly dressing in white coveralls and blue plastic booties. Two muzzled German shepherds on leashes were escorted from the K-9 vehicle by their male handler, a tall man who seemed too casually dressed for the occasion, in cream chinos and a navy baseball cap. A white tent was put up around the body, and the CSIs took it in turns to lug their equipment inside—big, ominous, bulging black satchels. They moved rhythmically, like this was habitual, ordinary, just another day at the office. But for Ali, this was the craziest thing she'd ever experienced.

Just then, the female detective paced across the sand toward the huddle of witnesses. She was dressed head to toe in black—high-heeled black boots, black skinny jeans, black leather jacket—all of which seemed like an odd choice to Ali considering they were in the height of the California summer.

"Detective Elton," the woman announced. Her voice was deep and husky. "Who was the first to find the body?"

The fisherman identified himself, raising his hand like a school child. He looked traumatized, with the hollow-eyed expression of a haunted man.

With a tip of the head, Detective Elton beckoned him to her. He broke from the huddle, scurrying to her obediently.

As Detective Elton set about taking down his statement, Ali checked her watch. Barely thirty minutes had passed since that piercing scream had broken the morning's tranquility, but each minute had felt like an hour. She wondered how long she'd have to stay here. She needed to get to open the bakery; it would look bad for her business if she opened late on her second day. She shifted uncomfortably from foot to foot, her legs cramping. Without meaning to, she let out a deep yawn.

"Is there somewhere more important you need to be?" a sharp, chastising voice said.

Ali's gaze snapped up. Detective Elton was glaring at her.

"No," Ali said, guiltily. "Sorry."

The detective narrowed her eyes. "Come here. I want to take your statement next."

"M—me?" Ali stammered. "I don't think I'll be much help."

"I'll be the judge of that," Detective Elton replied.

Ali gulped. Detective Elton was intimidating to say the least. She had the fierceness of a school principal, mixed with the appearance of a Gotham City baddie.

Tentatively, Ali left the relative comfort of the neon-clad power walkers and approached the detective. As she drew up in front of her, she realized they were in full view of the pier, which had begun winding up for the day. The food kiosks were selling waffles and fried donuts to visitors, who'd probably driven to the beach early for the peace and quiet of the morning, and were now crowded along the railings looking down at the unfolding horror beneath them. Ali felt scrutinized under their gazes. Judged. Even though she was an innocent bystander and they were the ones who'd chosen to gawk at a dead man over breakfast.

Ali was also aware of the audience forming outside the stores on the boardwalk. These were her neighbors, her peers, people she'd not yet even had a chance to properly meet. And now every one of them had a front row seat, watching on as the new girl from the bakery was questioned by the cops. Detective Elton couldn't have chosen a more exposed location to take Ali's statement if she'd tried. Ali wondered if that was the point.

"Let's start with the basics," Detective Elton said. "Name?"

"Allison Sweet."

The detective raised a single eyebrow. "Sweet? Really?"

Ali felt her hackles rise. She was about to make a quip about having inherited the name from her father, but decided against it. Detective Elton didn't seem like the kind of person who appreciated humor.

"Okay…" the detective said, sounding nonplussed. "Address?"

Ali pointed into the distance, to the bright blue door of her beachside bungalow.

"Over there," she said.

The detective looked up from her notepad. She seemed just as unimpressed with this answer as she had with Ali's name. Ali could tell she'd rubbed her the wrong way, though she had no idea why.

"Tell me what happened this morning," Detective Elton said.

"I've no idea," Ali replied. "He was dead when I got here."

"What time was that?"

Ali shrugged. "Some time after dawn."

Detective Elton's brown eyes narrowed. "Can you be more precise?"

"Sixish? Sevenish? What time is it now? I think you guys arrived about fifteen minutes after me."

Detective Elton snapped her notebook shut and glowered at Ali. "I think you ought to be taking this a bit more seriously. A man is dead under suspicious circumstances and—"

"—Suspicious?" Ali echoed. "You mean you think he was…" She lowered her voice. "…murdered?"

"The large blow to his head would suggest foul play, yes," Detective Elton replied, thinly.

Ali felt queasy all of a sudden. This might well all be par for the course for the police, but for her, a pastry chef, murder was a whole other thing. To think a murderer was wandering the streets of Willow Bay. And she thought she'd been having bad luck…

"Did you know the deceased?" the detective asked.

Ali hesitated. Did their one short, shouty interaction count?

She decided it didn't. It was probably unwise to tell the cops she and the dead guy had had a bust up less than half a day earlier.

She shook her head. "I'm pretty new around here. I've just opened a bakery, you see. In fact, yesterday was my first day. Hey, you should come by when you're done here. For breakfast. You and the rest of the crime scene investigators. I'll do a cop discount." She smiled.

Detective Elton blinked at Ali, as if not sure what to make of her. Her face remained blank. Then she turned and walked away, without so much as a farewell.

Left standing in the middle of the beach alone, Ali looked left and right, not sure what she was supposed to do next. Then she spotted the male detective on his way over to her. He was short, almost boyish in his appearance, with a pug nose and round, button-like brown eyes. He reminded Ali of a Boy Scout in his crisp white button-up shirt.

"Miss Sweet?" he asked.

Ali nodded. "That's right. I gave my statement to your partner."

"Oh, it's not about that," he said, sounding almost sheepish. "I heard you're offering a cop discount on breakfast today?"

"Yes!" Ali exclaimed. "Come by when you're done. All of you. Coffee's on the house."

He opened his mouth to respond but didn't get a chance, because Detective Elton shouted across the beach, "Callihan!"

"I'd better go," Detective Callihan said, turning back to his crew. "Hey, everyone, free coffee at Seaside Sweets as soon as we are done here!"

"See you later," Ali said, hopefully, as he scurried away. "I hope."

If she couldn't even entice a bunch of exhausted cops with free coffee, then her bakery was surely doomed.

CHAPTER FIFTEEN

Ali drummed her fingers nervously on the countertop. It had been a couple of hours since she'd been on the beach with the cops, and not a single customer had entered all morning.

She sunk her head into her hands, feeling demoralized. If she couldn't even give away coffee then she really was screwed.

Just then, the bell over the door chimed and she glanced up to see preppy Boy Scout Detective Callihan entering. Filing in behind was a stream of crime scene investigators. They'd changed out of their protective white overalls, and were in beige police cargo pants and navy polo tops. As they crowded inside and took over the window seats, it took all of Ali's self-control not to jump for joy.

"Detective Callihan," she said, adopting a courteous tone to mask her fizzing excitement. "You brought the troops."

He flashed her a tired smile, and dimples appeared in his puppy-fat cheeks. "We're desperate for caffeine."

Ali noticed the purple bags beneath his eyes.

"I'm not surprised," she said. "You must've woken at the crack of dawn. Are you all done down on the beach?"

He nodded. "It's the crime scene cleaners' turn."

Ali tried not to imagine what that may involve, and busied herself prepping the coffee machine with fresh beans. It was a professional barista machine that she'd bought secondhand from a closing down café and hadn't yet mastered.

"How many am I making?" she asked.

Detective Callihan used an index finger to count the array of men and women sitting shoulder to shoulder at the window tables. "Eleven."

"And do you want pastries with your coffee?" Ali asked.

"Me?" the detective replied. "No, no. I don't do carbs." He patted his stomach.

Why doesn't anybody do carbs anymore? Ali thought, desperately.

"But I'd better get something for that lot. It's the least I can do. There aren't many perks in their line of work."

Ali felt a spark of excitement as Detective Callihan fished his credit card out of the pocket of his cargo pants.

"So, ten pastries?" she asked, hopefully.

"Better make it fifteen," he said. He lowered his voice. "Some of them have large appetites."

Ali gestured to the fridge display. "Take your pick."

Detective Callihan bent down and peered at all the array of French pastries available, from chocolate eclairs to gold-dusted profiteroles, the mille-feuilles and canelés, and Ali's personal favorite—a perfectly presented Croquembouche in their delicate crispy caramel netting.

"Em..." Detective Callihan said with uncertainty. "I don't even know how to pronounce half of these." He straightened up, his cheeks pink with embarrassment. "Maybe you should pick."

"Sure," Ali said.

She punched the sale into her mini card reader for the first time ever, her hands trembling slightly from excitement, then Detective Callihan tapped his card and the sale went through with a simple bleep that sounded as joyful to Ali's ears as Santa's sleigh bells to a kid on Christmas.

"Take a seat," she said, outwardly keeping her composure despite her fluttering stomach. "I'll bring them over."

"Thanks," Detective Callihan said.

He headed off to join the rest of his team.

As soon as he was gone, Ali turned and discreetly punched the air. She'd made a sale! Her first! Of course, she hadn't actually made a profit, because she'd given away the coffee (her most expensive item) for free, but that was beside the point. She'd made a sale! And if the officers liked the pastries, maybe they'd come back for more another day. With their spouses. Their kids. Grandma, grandad, and the rest of the extended family...

Ali knew she was getting a little bit away with herself. She tried to rein in her excitement as she made the coffees and selected a range of pastries, presenting them beautifully on several plates. She brought the lot over to the table on a big tray, the crime scene investigators looking up as she approached.

"Croissants!" a woman with dyed red hair and a silver nose stud said eagerly.

The rather large man beside her licked his lips hungrily.

"Is this on you, boss?" he asked Detective Callihan through a big bushy brown beard.

The detective looked coy as he smiled his dimpled smile. "Yup."

The investigators applauded.

They seemed like a jovial group, Ali thought. Which was impressive considering they earned their salaries by prodding dead bodies.

She began transferring the coffees off the tray to the customers on the first table. As she did, she couldn't help but overhear the conversation of the investigators on the next table over.

"His injuries are definitely consistent with a fall," said one of the CSIs, a woman with glossy ginger hair.

"It wasn't a fall," a man with a shaved head countered. "For that kind of bruising, there needed to be some force behind it. It was a push."

"That's just conjecture," the first woman replied, shaking her glossy ginger mane. "You can't ascertain that from looking at the body. A slip from the pier could be equally plausible."

"The head wound was a deliberate blow," a third voice joined in with the fray, a young brunette with black-framed glasses. "The rest of the injuries were from the fall, or push, whichever you believe. But a blow came first."

The ginger-haired woman folded her arms. "We'll have to wait and see what the pathologist's report says. All we can be sure of is that from the lividity and stage of rigor mortis, the death occurred yesterday evening."

Evening, Ali thought, as she handed a steaming black coffee to the bright and expectant-looking dyed-red-haired woman.

Evening was a slightly vague time frame, open to interpretation. For Ali, evening was the time you ate dinner, so anywhere between six and ten. Which meant the victim may well have been killed when she was taking her solo pier stroll...

The realization hit Ali like a ton of bricks. She might've walked past the murderer! Heck, she might've been murdered herself if the timing had been slightly different! She'd just had a major brush with death!

Her legs went weak, and she stumbled, almost knocking the tray that was still half full of coffees and pastries.

Detective Callihan was out of his seat in a second, jumping to her aid so quickly the chair squeaked.

"Are you all right?" he asked, catching her by the elbow.

"I'm fine," Ali replied, breathlessly. But she wasn't. Her heart was going like a jackhammer. Her head felt light, like she was about to faint.

"Maybe you should sit down," Detective Callihan suggested gently. Ali nodded.

The CSI agents watched on with concern as Detective Callihan guided her away from the window. The feel of his fingers on her elbow was the only thing that actually felt real to Ali; the floor seemed to have turned to oatmeal.

He helped her over to a table, and she sank slowly into the seat. Nausea came to join her racing heart and spinning head.

"Let me fetch you some water," Detective Callihan said.

But Ali shook her head. "I'm fine. Thank you. I feel better now I'm sitting."

Detective Callihan took the seat opposite her, peering at her like a doctor with a patient. "Are you sure? You've gone pale. Have you eaten today? It may be low blood sugar."

"It's not that," Ali confessed. "I overheard your team talking. About how that man died. How they think someone pushed him from the pier. I realized how it could've been me because I was there."

Detective Callihan's face dropped. He looked suddenly mortified. He glanced over his shoulder at the CSIs chatting away and eating pastries.

"Please keep what you heard in the strictest of confidence," he said, turning back to her with serious eyes. "I can't stress this enough. If you tell anyone, it may jeopardize the entire investigation."

"I won't," Ali told him. "I promise."

He nodded curtly. "Thank you." Then a line appeared between his brows. "Wait. Did you say you were there?"

Ali nodded. "Yesterday evening, after work. I went for a walk along the pier alone."

At the same moment the words left her lips, the door swung open and in strode the black-clad Detective Elton.

The vibe in the bakery changed immediately. Silence descended.

The formidable woman stood in the doorway, assessing the scene through her sunglasses. She looked from Ali in her chair to Detective Callihan leaning toward her, his elbows on his knees. He immediately sat back. Then, as if on second thought, he stood and took a step away from Ali.

Ali couldn't bear the tension.

"Are you here for a free coffee?" she asked Detective Elton, hopefully.

Detective Elton pushed her sunglasses onto her head and peered down at her suspiciously.

"Did I just hear you say you were on the pier last night?" she asked in her smoky voice, ignoring the question.

Ali gulped and nodded.

Detective Elton made a shoo gesture to Detective Callihan. He obediently scurried away and joined the hushed CSIs in the window.

From the breast pocket of her leather biker jacket, Detective Elton removed a notebook and pen. "Tell me about last night," she commanded.

Ali shifted uncomfortably. "I went for a walk after work," she offered.

"Time?" Detective Elton asked.

"About seven," Ali said.

"Reason?"

"Reason?" Ali echoed. "I guess I'd had a bad day and wanted a bit of alone time, you know? Some time to reflect. To look at the ocean and the moon and think about, you know, existence…"

Detective Elton looked up from her notebook, nonplussed. Clearly, she wasn't a woman who spent much time pondering existence.

Ali squirmed in her seat.

"Why didn't you mention this in your statement?" Detective Elton asked.

"It didn't occur to me to," Ali explained. "I didn't know he'd been pushed from the pier back then."

She shuddered, and her stomach churned with nausea all over again.

Suddenly furious, Detective Elton snapped her notebook shut and glared at Detective Callihan. He appeared even younger and more boyish shrinking back from her glare.

Ali suddenly realized what she'd done. When Detective Callihan had asked her to keep quiet, he'd meant from *everyone*—Detective Elton included. She'd just tattled on him by accident. By the look of Detective Elton's furious expression, Ali had just landed him right in it.

Detective Elton's cold gaze swept over the party of CSIs, from their half-drunk coffees, to the selection of prettily presented pastries.

"Everyone out," she commanded.

They didn't need telling twice. They were on their feet in a matter of seconds, filing for the door. Detective Callihan brought up the rear, looking extremely sheepish. Detective Elton stopped him with a hand.

"This is completely inappropriate," she said through her teeth.

Ali felt the need to defend Detective Callihan. The poor man had only been trying to boost his team's morale after a grueling early-morning shift, and now Ali had gotten him in trouble with his superior.

"It was my fault," Ali piped up. "I'm nosy. That's all. And if you think about it, it worked out for the best because I might be an important witness now."

Detective Elton narrowed her eyes. Ali realized, with sudden panic, that she wasn't looking at her like an important witness, but as a suspect.

Oh crap, she thought.

Ali had seen enough cop shows to know that there were three things the cops looked for to pinpoint a suspect: means, motive, and opportunity. By placing herself at the scene of a murder without an alibi, she'd just put a huge check mark next to opportunity.

Detective Elton continued her aside to Detective Callihan. "We just got a positive ID on the victim. Preston Lockley. Lives in the orange house up the hill."

Her tone was equivalent to a click of the fingers.

Detective Callihan mumbled, "Thanks for the coffee," over his shoulder at Ali, then scampered out into the sunshine with the rest of the CSIs.

Panic overcame Ali as she realized she hadn't ticked one box, but two. There had been witnesses to her and the victim, Preston Lockley's, altercation—he'd yelled at her as he left her shop. That gave her a motive. Revenge. Retribution. Score-settling.

So not only did she have the opportunity, she also had a motive. The only thing missing was the means—which, of course, they wouldn't find because she hadn't hit him over the head with anything. But the CSIs had said his injuries could be consistent with a fall. So if his death hadn't been caused by the blow but by drowning, caused by the killer's push, well, that was something very much within Ali's abilities. That gave her the third and final check.

"Ms. Sweet," Detective Elton said, peering at her intently. "You're not planning on leaving Willow Bay anytime soon, are you?"

Ali swallowed the anxious lump in her throat. Her mouth was too dry to speak, so she shook her head.

"Good," Detective Elton replied, tipping her sunglasses back down to the bridge of her nose. "It's best you stick around town."

She gave the store a final, parting look of distaste, then left.

Ali sunk her head into her hands. How had she ended up in such a mess?

CHAPTER SIXTEEN

With a sigh of defeat, Ali swept her unsold pastries into a carrier bag for the second night in a row. It wasn't yet five p.m., but she'd decided to close up shop early. She had been preemptive in her joy at having made her first sale. After Detective Elton had ordered her team out, the store had remained empty for the rest of the day. She'd not even had a kid come in to use the restroom, or a seagull steal her croissants.

She decided to visit Delaney, and took her cell phone out of her pocket so she could have a Teddy pep talk on the way there.

She paused with her thumb hovering over the dial button. Teddy had blabbed all her secrets to Hannah. If he couldn't keep quiet about her ex-boyfriend being gay, he certainly wouldn't be able to hold out about a dead body washing up on the beach mere yards from her home. Hannah would obviously tell their mom, and their mom would probably go all Momma-Bear and drive to Willow Bay to kidnap Ali back home. In this day and age of the internet and twenty-four-hour news cycles, Ali knew it wouldn't take long before they found out, but she wanted to delay that moment for as long as humanly possible.

She put her cell phone back in her pocket and turned to lock the door.

With her back turned, Ali heard the rhythmic footsteps of a group of joggers passing behind her.

"That's her," a female voice whispered. "The new girl."

"You mean the murderer?" came an equally hushed reply.

Ali froze, horrified that they thought she was responsible for Preston's murder. She fiddled with her keys, pretending to still be doing something, so she could avoid turning back around.

But the group slowed their pace, presumably to get a better look at the supposed murderer, and Ali felt chills run up and down her spine at their continued gossip.

"She doesn't look like the type," said another whispered voice.

Ali stayed in her frozen position, her ears burning with fury, until the joggers had finally gone. She stashed her keys in her pocket and marched in the direction of Delaney's store.

She'd never felt so desperate for a friend to talk to.

As the pier loomed into view, Ali was surprised to see the pier still open to the public. It was less busy than it had been yesterday, because no doubt most folk were planning on avoiding it for a little while, but it was open for business nonetheless. In fact, the only area still cordoned off with police tape was near the end of the pier.

Despite the warmth of the evening, goosebumps appeared on Ali's arms as she thought about Preston Lockley and what had become of him. The cordoned area included the Ferris wheel, where Ali had been standing just twenty-four hours earlier. Had his body been there when she had, floating in the ocean just yards below the spot she'd stood? Or had he been pushed later, after she'd left? Either way, the thought turned her stomach.

A flash of red interrupted her ruminations. She followed the streak with her eyes. It was Django the monkey in his red and gold silk outfit, scurrying from one tourist to the next in an attempt to lure them into Lavinia's dark green, wooden caravan.

Ali hunkered down and hastened her step. The last thing she needed right now was to be accosted by the fortune teller's monkey.

But no one got past Django, and the furry critter skidded to a halt in front of her.

She looked at him. He looked at her. Then he bared his teeth, hissed, and ran away.

Wow, Ali thought. *Even the monkey won't mess with me.*

She stuffed her hands deeper into her pockets and hurried onward.

Soon, she passed Miriyam's store, *Kookies.* Unlike her own bakery, Miryiam's was brimming with customers. On the chalkboard behind where the woman stood, there was a freshly chalked advertisement for a special new cookie. She'd called it the Killer Kookie, and the tag line read: Kookies to Die For.

Ali grimaced at how crass and disrespectful the marketing gimmick was.

Just then, Miriyam caught her glowering through the windows, and her eyebrow twitched up questioningly. She narrowed her brown eyes with accusation.

Ali scurried away.

She was relieved to enter the relative safety of Little Bits of This and That. The craft store was as beautifully put together as its owner, with a large table for craft parties, and all kinds of delightfully presented shelves of yarn, fabric, and ribbons. If anyone could make crafting look like a legit hobby for someone older than twelve, it would be the gorgeous Delaney.

The woman herself was sitting at her counter, operating a sewing machine as gracefully as someone playing a concert piano. It buzzed and whirred as she worked, no doubt crafting some amazingly creative and unique object with her exceptional talent.

When Delaney spotted Ali lingering in the doorway, she gasped and jumped up. Her beaded jewelry rattled as she hurried toward Ali and wrapped her up in her arms. She even smelled beautiful, like fragrant spices being cooked in a field of fresh heather.

"Oh, Ali!" she exclaimed. "I heard what happened with Preston. Isn't it awful?"

Ali shuddered as the visual memories from earlier that morning flashed through her mind like some kind of horror movie slideshow. "Unfortunately, I had a front row seat to all the drama."

"Well, don't worry," Delaney said, studying her face with crystal-blue eyes framed by perfectly shaped brows. "I don't believe a word of those nasty rumors being spread around about you."

Ali felt her face blanch. She opened her mouth to ask what exactly Delaney had heard, but didn't get the chance because Delaney took her by the shoulders and steered her toward the craft table.

"Come. Sit down!" she said, plonking Ali into a seat surrounded by mini bottles of glitter.

Evidently, Delaney's customer base was still hungry for crafting, despite the recent goings-on. Ali wished she wasn't surrounded by a million scattered googly eyes that seemed to be judging her.

Delaney leaned her head on her fist and peered at Ali, her sea-blue eyes conveying both curiosity and trustworthiness. "So what are you going to do?"

"I honestly don't know," Ali said. "I mean, I was on the pier last night about the time he was killed. I was alone. I have no alibi for the time of the killing."

"Well, neither do I!" Delaney exclaimed, so loudly she made Ali jump and accidentally stick her elbow into a pot of glitter. "Nor does every romantically unattached person in Willow Bay. Goodness. I'm sure they're not going to accuse every singleton, are they?"

She chuckled. She was evidently trying to be reassuring, but it wasn't working. Ali felt paranoid, like the whole town was turning against her.

"It's not just that." Ali continued brushing a flat palm over the glitter now stuck to her shirt with futility; she knew full well from Teddy's Pride Parades she'd be shedding glitter for the next month. "Preston had been in my store earlier that evening. Literally an hour or something before he died. Which means I might well have been the last person he interacted with before he was murdered. And a whole bunch of people witnessed our argument about the lease."

Ali's chest sank. She couldn't help but feel personally responsible about the whole debacle, even though she'd had no idea about Preston's agreement with Kerrigan, and hadn't realized she'd undercut him.

Delaney leaned across the craft table and gave Ali's forearm a reassuring shake.

"This will pass," she said. "And you're far too sweet to be a killer. I mean, your name is literally Sweet. The police will see that soon enough." She patted her hand. "I'm going to make some tea. Chamomile. Helps calm the nerves." She stood and floated toward the backroom kitchen. "Why don't you do some coloring while you're waiting? It can be very therapeutic. Use your non-dominant hand. It's a scientifically proven anxiety-busting technique!" Then she disappeared out of sight.

Ali slumped back in her chair, mulling on her misery. She picked up the coloring sheet closest at hand. It was, aptly, of a cake decorated with hearts and stars. She grabbed the pink pencil, put it in her left hand, and got to work on the hearts.

How had she ended up in such a mess? As the prime suspect in a murder? This was so far from the dream life she'd come here chasing. Her cute little seaside town would forever be tainted by this horrible event.

Delaney returned.

"How are you getting on?" she asked as she placed a bright teapot on the table. Floral and herbal scents radiated from it.

Ali looked down at her coloring. Her pink cake was a mess to say the least. But Delaney's technique had been surprisingly effective. Non-dominant hand coloring *was* calming.

"Did you know Preston?" Ali asked as Delaney poured the tea.

Delaney shook her head. "Not really."

"What does that mean?"

"Well, I mean, everyone knew Preston Lockley. You didn't need to know him personally to know of him."

"I don't understand," Ali replied.

Delaney paused, looking uncomfortable. Even her expression of discomfort was pretty.

"He was the local weirdo," she explained, before hurriedly adding, "but who gets to decide what's normal and what isn't anyway? I spend all day working with glitter and glue!" She laughed nervously and buried her face in her teacup as she sipped.

Ali frowned. "Why was he the local weirdo?"

Delaney shrugged. "He still lived with his mom."

"Plenty of people still live with their mom," Ali pressed. "LA rents are crazy."

Delaney looked under pressure. She put her cup on the saucer and spoke in a low voice, even though they were the only people in the store. "He had an obsession."

Ali's eyes widened. "With women?"

"No." Delaney shook her head. "Balloons."

Ali frowned. *Balloons?* She'd not been expecting that.

"What kind of obsession?" she asked.

Delaney gave a little shrug. "Just, you know, an obsession. Hot air balloons. Helium balloons. He made a film about the Hindenburg disaster. Claymation." She sipped her tea. "But I don't think we should judge him for any of that stuff. Especially not now he's passed."

It was curious to say the least. And Delaney was right. Who were they to judge the victim for his peculiar hobbies? It didn't make him any more deserving of his untimely death. And who was she to judge him for exploding at her in her store? If Kerrigan had done the same thing to her, she would've been furious too.

Ali put her pencil down with resolve. Whether it was the calming effects from the coloring task or the chamomile tea, or a side effect of whatever essential oil Delaney was pumping into the place, Ali decided she was going to get her dream life back. This thing was a blip. She'd been through worse. She would not let this crush her. If the police suspected her, then she would just have to investigate the murder herself and clear her name that way.

And she knew just the place to start.

She peered out the window at the steppingstones of rainbow houses until she found the orange one. The Lockley house.

CHAPTER SEVENTEEN

Ali woke at the usual time the next morning and headed to the bakery. She made an even smaller batch of breakfast pastries than yesterday to give herself time to make an apple pie—a part sympathy gift, part buttering up gift that she hoped would make Preston Lockley's mother more open to answering her questions. She waited out the customerless breakfast shift, then locked up and headed for the Lockleys' orange house.

The apple pie was still warm in her hands as she steeled herself and knocked on the door. She wasn't particularly happy about haranguing a grieving woman, but the only way she stood a chance of solving Preston's murder was to find out everything she could about him. Maybe he'd made some recent enemies. The sort of guy who shouted at people he didn't know had probably rubbed a few people the wrong way over the years. And no one would know about that stuff better than the person he lived with, whom he saw on a day-to-day basis, which, in this case, happened to be his mother.

As she waited, the sun beat down on her, making sweat bead on the back of her neck. She heard shuffling footsteps from the other side. The door was opened by a short Asian woman in green scrubs. Ali guessed she was a nurse of some type.

"Yes?" the woman asked.

"I'm so sorry to disturb you," Ali said, using the overly formal newsreader voice she often slipped into when nervous. "I was wondering if Preston's mother was here? I wanted to pay my respects." She held up the apple pie dish to emphasize the point.

The Asian woman looked nonplussed. Her gaze slid down to the pie, widened with hunger, then rose back up again to meet Ali's eyes. "We've had quite a lot of food dropped around already. I don't know if there's room left in the fridge for it."

"It can sit at room temperature," Ali explained. "No fridge needed." She smiled hopefully.

The Asian woman didn't smile in return. But she nodded and opened the door wider. "Fine. Come in."

"Thank you," Ali said.

She stepped inside, onto a grubby mint green carpet. The decor of the home was dated, with faded balloon motif wallpaper that looked like it was intended for a children's bedroom, and framed family photographs covered in a thin layer of dust.

"Genevieve's in there," the Asian nurse said, pointing through to the living room. "I'll get plates."

"Thanks," Ali said.

The nurse disappeared down the corridor.

Ali steeled herself with a breath, then stepped into the living room.

The decor was dated in here as well. The couch and armchair looked faded and raggedy. The pale green carpet was completely flattened by years of footfall. Despite the bright day, thick cream curtains were drawn across the windows, and the only light in the room came from a bulb overhead, which was almost entirely suffocated out by a large, tasseled lampshade. This, Ali realized, was what grief looked like.

She spotted the woman then, Genevieve Lockley, the mother of a murdered son. She was sitting in the armchair, her gray hair flattened against the white lace doily headrest. She didn't look old enough for care visits—seventy, at a push. Ali wondered about the nurse clattering around in the kitchen. Was she here because Genevieve was too grief-stricken to care for herself at the moment? Or did Mrs. Lockley have some other kind of ailment that required personal home care?

"Mrs. Lockley?" Ali asked tentatively.

The woman looked over her shoulder at the stranger standing in her living room. Her pale gray eyes were vacant, like there was no one behind them. A wan smile tugged up the corner of her thin lips.

"Hello, Bess," she said.

"Oh," Ali said, tiptoeing into the dim light. "I'm not Bess. I'm Ali."

The woman frowned. "From church?"

"From the bakery. Seaside Sweets. Do you know it?"

Genevieve's frown only deepened. "No."

Of course she doesn't know it, Ali scolded herself. *No one does!*

"What are you holding?" Genevieve demanded.

Ali sensed her presence was less than welcome.

"Pie," she said, sheepishly, raising the dish up in both hands. "I thought you might want a little pick-me-up. Do you like pie?"

"Of course I do," came the woman's abrupt reply. "Who doesn't like pie?"

In this town, Ali thought, *apparently everyone…*

"Sit down!" Genevieve Lockley commanded.

Ali quickly obliged. She placed the pie down on the coffee table, which was a lacquered wooden block that screamed 1970s, then perched uncomfortably on the edge of the couch, as if ready to flee at a moment's notice.

Up close, she could see Genevieve was far from elderly. She looked a similar age to Ali's own mother, who'd just turned sixty. "Sixty years young," as she liked to say. Georgia Sweet still did weekly Zumba classes. She had regular hairdresser appointments to keep her grays at bay. She even owned pleather pants (much to Ali's embarrassment). She wouldn't be seen dead in an armchair with a lace doily behind her head. Ali deduced there was something wrong with Genevieve Lockley, beyond her grief.

"What flavor is it?" Genevieve asked.

"Apple."

"Apple?" She scoffed. "That's the worst kind."

Just then, the nurse came into the room. She placed three porcelain plates on the coffee table, and three forks clattered beside them. She got to work carving up the pie.

"Who did you say you were again?" she asked, as she dumped a plate in Ali's lap.

"I didn't," Ali said.

"It's Bess!" Genevieve exclaimed. "From church!"

The Asian woman flashed Ali a knowing look. "We're all Bess from church."

Ali shifted uncomfortably. This hadn't been what she was expecting when she'd come here. She thought she would be talking to a grieving mother, but instead she'd found a confused woman and a nurse in scrubs as an audience member.

The nurse handed Genevieve her slice of pie, then took a whopping great slice for herself. She flopped down onto the couch beside Ali.

"So, Bess from church, who are you really?" she asked.

She had an interrogative way of speaking, which took Ali aback.

"I run the new bakery," she explained. "Seaside Sweets. My name's Ali."

"And you knew Preston?" the nurse continued.

"Sort of. I met him once before he died."

Just then, Genevieve let out a huge gasp. "Preston's dead?"

Ali's eyes widened with horror. She didn't know? No one had told her that her son was dead?

But then Genevieve frowned and added, "Who's Preston?"

Ali exhaled all in one go. It finally fell into place. Genevieve had Alzheimer's.

The nurse answered Genevieve's question by pointing her fork at a family photograph on the wall, which showed Preston and his mother holding a big bunch of balloons.

"Balloon man!" Genevieve exclaimed.

Genevieve's Alzheimer's must be rather progressed, Ali thought, if she was unable to remember her own son, or his death the day earlier. That meant Genevieve Lockley wasn't the person who knew Preston the best, because her own brain was eroding her memories of him. Coming here was a mistake.

Ali put her pie on the lacquered table, ready to apologize and leave, when she noticed Mrs. Lockley's gaze had changed. As she looked at the photograph of her son and his balloons, her eyes became bright, alert. She seemed suddenly present.

Ali paused. She'd heard about this, how some Alzheimer's patients would slip in and out of lucidity. Maybe coming here hadn't been a mistake after all.

"A lovely man," Genevieve continued, speaking with her mouth full of pie. "A lovely man." She looked at her nurse. "Did he ever open his store?"

The Asian nurse's cheeks bulged with the apple pie she was devouring. "The landlord didn't want him," she said, loudly, spraying crumbs down the front of her green apron. She looked at Ali. "Did you make this? It's good."

"Uh, yeah," Ali said, absentmindedly, only half listening because her full attention was on Genevieve. The woman's expression had soured the instant she'd heard the word *landlord*, and Ali's curiosity was piqued.

"Do you know Kerrigan?" Ali asked the woman.

Genevieve forked some pie into her mouth. "Kerrigan O'Neal? He's a nasty man. I never liked him. All poor Preston ever wanted to do was open a balloon store of his own and that man just kept saying no."

"He refused him?" Ali asked.

This was news to her. Back when Preston had barged into her store to accuse her of undercutting him, Ali had just assumed he'd struck a deal with Kerrigan, one she'd accidentally interrupted.

"Every time," Genevieve said.

"Trust me when I say there were a *lot* of times," the nurse added as a wry aside. "He pestered Kerrigan constantly. Followed him around and around."

"Poor Preston," Genevieve said. "He had the money, but that nasty Kerrigan always said no."

"He never got over it," the nurse added.

Ali sank back against the couch, the revelation percolating through her mind. So the deal she thought she'd ruined between Kerrigan and Preston had never even existed in the first place? There was no contract after Pete's Pitas had vacated the premises that she'd accidentally trampled on. Preston had been pestering Kerrigan for the lease for years, by the sounds of things, and had always been turned down.

Ali wondered why. Kerrigan had seemed eager to get the lease off his hands when she'd called him. She'd watched him practically run out of his yellow house to meet her. He'd snapped up Teddy's offer with barely any back and forth, like he'd been desperate for someone, anyone, to sign on the dotted line. And yet all along, he'd had a very eager and willing person in Preston.

Ali needed to find out more. And she knew exactly who to speak to next.

CHAPTER EIGHTEEN

Ali went up the hill to the canary yellow door of her landlord, Kerrigan O'Neal, and knocked. There was still a couple of hours before the usual mid-morning lull would turn to lunchtime, so Ali didn't feel much of a pressing need to get back to her store any time soon.

The door clicked open and Ali's stout landlord stood before her. He was wearing muddy boots and gardening gloves, and had the same blustery aura of their first meeting, like he'd just been interrupted in the middle of a very pressing task.

"Allison?" Kerrigan said, sliding the gloves off and holding them in his hands. "Is everything okay with the store? The apartment?"

"They're both fine," Ali said. "I just wanted to ask you something. Is now a bad time?"

"No, no, I'm just doing some gardening," Kerrigan replied, waving the gloves as proof. "What did you want to ask?"

"It's about Preston Lockley," Ali said, watching carefully for any change in Kerrigan's demeanor.

Kerrigan tutted and shook his head. "Preston. Shocking. Terrible. It's hard to believe something so awful can happen in a town like this."

"I heard he wanted to rent my store before me," Ali said. "And that you turned him down?"

Kerrigan looked uncomfortable, his gaze darting over Ali's shoulders to scan the street behind her.

"Maybe we should talk inside?" he said.

Ali faltered. She'd expected this to be a quick chat, with Kerrigan explaining his reasons for turning Preston's offer down. But something about his mannerisms made her uncomfortable. A tingly sensation spread through her.

"I guess we can talk while you garden, if you want," Ali said.

Kerrigan looked surprised, as if multi-tasking was a novel idea Ali had just invented. Maybe that was one of the reasons he always seemed so blustering.

"That's a good idea," he said, opening the door wider to allow her inside.

Apprehensively, Ali stepped in.

Kerrigan's house was bigger than she'd expected looking at it from the front, but three-story townhouses always seemed to be optical illusions. She followed him along a corridor with high ceilings, and into a large, bright kitchen, with enormous windows that looked out onto a steeply banked garden, stretching for yards up to a dividing fence and the back of the next big rainbow house on the hill. It gave Ali a peculiar combination of claustrophobia and vertigo.

"Wow, you don't get much privacy on the hill, do you?" Ali commented, peering up to the next house where she could easily see in through the French doors at the back to their kitchen. She was, of course, just as easily visible to them.

Kerrigan chuckled. "You wouldn't be able to hide a body in the garden, that's for sure."

Ali didn't quite know what to make of that. Off-color jokes didn't seem particularly advisable considering the circumstances. And her hackles were already up.

"Sorry, that's what we say in Ireland," he added.

Ali reminded herself to Google that later.

Kerrigan gestured to a wooden bench, and Ali sat. Then he hitched up his trousers, crouched, and began weeding a flower bed full of wildflowers that were luring in numerous bee and butterfly visitors.

"So you want to know about Preston?" he asked, his focus on the task at hand.

He sounded weary, like he'd been anticipating the conversation. Ali felt even more on edge, like she was on the cusp of learning some big secret.

"That's right," she said, her voice quivering slightly. "He was supposed to lease the store before me, right? Before I undercut him."

Kerrigan said nothing. For a moment, the sound of his trowel entering the earth was the only noise.

"You didn't undercut him," he said, finally. "Because I never had any intentions to rent to him in the first place. I wouldn't trust the man to water my plants, let alone run a successful business. A balloon store would've folded within the first month, and then I'd have to find someone else to take over the lease. Assuming I was even able to evict him, that is. The sort of man who still lives in his mother's home at forty isn't the sort of person I can imagine leaving without a fuss."

Kerrigan clearly didn't have any qualms about talking ill of the dead. Ali wondered if that was an Irish thing as well.

93

"He seemed to think differently," Ali said. "According to him, there was a deal."

Kerrigan's hunched shoulders gave off the impression her questions were flustering him.

"I might have… implied something of the sort," he mumbled.

Ali frowned. "What do you mean?"

Kerrigan turned. "Look. Preston was a pest, okay? He must've asked me a million times for a lease for that blasted balloon store. Sometimes the only way to get him off my back was to bend the truth a bit."

Ali narrowed her eyes. "You told him you would one day."

He let out a big sigh. "I told him that if Pete's Pitas ever closed down, I'd rent to him. Because I never, ever thought Pete would close that place. I know. I'm not proud of it. It was a cowardly thing to do. But he pushed me to the end of my tether, really."

Ali wanted to ask him why he hadn't warned her about Preston. If the man had been so relentless in his pursuit of a lease, Kerrigan must've anticipated she'd soon be getting the brunt of his anger. At the very least her landlord could have warned her to expect a visit from him so she could prepare herself. If she'd known Preston had been harassing him for years, she would never have even entertained the theory that he'd thrown himself off the pier because of her undercutting him! It would've saved her a whole lot of grief and anxiety.

But Ali held her tongue, because she wanted to give Kerrigan the space to explain himself.

"I'm not proud of what I did," her landlord said in a low voice. "I should've stayed firm and just said no. I didn't think it would come to… this."

Ali instantly knew what Kerrigan meant. He'd heard the gossip going around town that the new bakery lady had killed Preston Lockley after a vicious argument witnessed outside her store. And since that argument had essentially been caused by Kerrigan himself for leading Preston to believe he actually had a chance of taking on the lease, he was clearly carrying some of the burden of blame. It took all of Ali's patience not to tell him that fact. Because who could've possibly imagined it would come to this?

"Why were you so dead set against leasing to him?" she asked. "A balloon store doesn't seem like such a terrible idea to me. This is a tourist town after all. There are plenty of kids around with parents' arms to twist. Why would a balloon store be such an obvious failure?"

Kerrigan sighed. "Beyond him lowballing below the asking price?" He shifted uncomfortably. "I thought he was weird. He gave off creepy vibes." He became more quiet. "Put quite simply, I just didn't like him."

Ali pondered his words. From what she'd learned so far about Preston Lockley, he'd been unanimously unpopular in Willow Bay. The local weirdo. But beyond being upset about Kerrigan misleading him and taking it out on Ali, she'd heard no concrete reason to justify everyone's dislike. It was as if they'd just decided he was a bad guy, in much the same way they'd all decided she was a killer. Poor Preston. Had he been ostracized by his entire community for no reason? And did the same fate now await her?

Ali cast her mind back to that moment in the store. Preston had been furious with her, accusing her of undermining his deal with Kerrigan. But what had happened after he'd left? All she knew for certain was that shortly after, he'd ended up on the pier. What had he been doing there? What had happened between the time he was yelling at her and the time he'd ended up floating in the ocean?

Ali didn't want to admit it to herself, but there was a strong chance the next person Preston had sought out after their altercation had been Kerrigan. He'd just discovered their supposed deal was a fraud, and after having shouted at the innocent victim in the whole debacle, who would he need to unleash his rage on next if not the man who'd deceived him in the first place? Was she really the last person to see Preston Lockley alive? Or had it been Kerrigan O'Neal...

Ali's heart began to race as she suddenly considered the terrible possibility she was sitting in the garden of a murderer. Kerrigan's shiftiness. His perpetual blusteriness. Was there more to Kerrigan O'Neal than met the eye? What if that old, tired argument between them turned explosive that night? That on the end of the pier, the two men had had a scuffle that escalated into murder?

Ali watched her landlord digging his garden aggressively, like he had a lot of stress to get out and only had the soil with which to release it.

"I heard he was killed on the pier," Ali said. She wanted to see whether she could provoke any kind of response in Kerrigan. "Pushed into the water."

Kerrigan didn't stop digging, though Ali noted a slight hesitancy in his movements. His shoulders appeared more hunched, like he was collapsing in on himself.

"I heard that too," he replied. "I always say those railings aren't high enough. If it's not the college kids on spring break diving off the end, it's things like this. People falling. There's a reason I don't let my kids go there, beyond that filthy monkey harboring diseases. It just doesn't seem safe."

He was blabbering.

Because he's nervous, Ali wondered, *or because he has something to hide?*

"You have kids?" she asked, trying to prompt more of Kerrigan's loose tongue.

"Yes. Three. And we prefer to get our amusements on dry land. They're too old for most of the stuff on the pier these days, anyway. Now it's all laser tag, which I'm much more partial to. Sad to think that while we were enjoying ourselves at LazerZone, a man was being murdered."

Ali paused. Kerrigan had just offered an alibi.

"LazerZone?" she asked.

"That's right." Kerrigan looked surprised she was showing an interest. "It's not far from here. Down the hill, on a side street off the boardwalk. You should try it some time."

"Maybe I will..." Ali said, conspiratorially.

Either Kerrigan was trying to double-bluff her, or the way he'd seamlessly plucked an alibi out of thin air without hesitation was his ticket to freedom.

She left Kerrigan's, realizing she needed to open her bakery soon. But Kerrigan had given her plenty to think about, and she couldn't help but strongly suspect he was hiding something from her. If his alibi proved to be fake, then she'd surely be on track to solve this whole case. Because if she didn't solve it soon, she'd have no store left to open, and her whole dream life in Willow Bay would collapse.

Ali was going to investigate his claims herself.

CHAPTER NINETEEN

LazerZone was very easy to find. It was a bright pink building with a huge flashing neon sign.

Ali pushed open the glass doors and headed inside.

It was dark, noisy, and smelled of dry ice mixed with sweaty bodies. To her right was a set of double doors, spray-painted a silvery color to look like industrial steel, complete with plastic bolts and a black and yellow striped hazard warning sign. A big red light flashed on and off above it to complete the effect.

The room was cleaved in half by a big reception desk, bright blue retro plastic like the ones Ali remembered from video stores before they all went bust. A surveillance camera screen was mounted in one corner, live-streaming the goings-on of the closed off arena. It looked a bit like a soft play area, with two floors connected by climbing nets and bridges and slides. A dozen or so feral kids were running amok inside the arena, bulky black belts around their waists, laser guns aloft, all dodging and shooting like they were soldiers in a futuristic war. There were so many flashing lights it gave Ali a headache just looking at the screen.

"Can I help?" a voice said.

Ali looked over to see a young, male staff member entering the reception room through the white connecting door. He was a redhead, and looked like he was only five minutes out of high school himself, barely older than the kids he was in charge of. A swath of angry red pimples covered the right side of his chin.

Ali stepped closer and tapped her fingers on the plastic counter dividing them. "Yes. I was wondering if you could tell me whether there was a man in here the other night. Kerrigan O'Neal."

The boy's ginger eyebrows came together in a frown.

"I can't tell you that," he said, folding his arms. "It's confidential."

Great. She'd managed to find the only teenage employee worried about ethics in LA.

She rummaged in her pocket and pulled out a crumpled dollar bill and a stick of gum, laying her bribe out on the countertop. "How about now?"

His eyes scanned the paltry offering. His expression was a combination of confusion, shock, and wariness.

"Do I need to call security?" he said.

Ali shook her head, thinking on her feet. What would Teddy do in this situation? Improvise!

She channeled the Valley Girls from her high school days. "Okay, like I totally get it. But, it's just like, I'm his niece, and I'm supposed to be throwing him a birthday party. And like, he totally loves LazerZone, but, like, I don't want to throw him a party if he's been here like, I don't know, in the last week or whatever. So can you, like, maybe just tell me if his name's in your booking system..." She squinted to read the name tag pinned to his bright blue polo shirt. "...Todd?"

She flashed her best airhead smile.

But Todd the Receptionist looked unimpressed. He gave his head a single, resolute shake.

"Sorry. Company policy. You'll have to ask him yourself."

"Like, I would, but it would totally spoil the surprise..."

It was useless. Valley Girl was getting her nowhere. Todd wasn't budging. She'd have to think of something else.

Just then, Ali spotted a visitor's sign-in book behind the ridge of the desk. If she could get Todd away from his desk, she'd be able to take a peek and find out for herself!

"Okay, well like, thanks, I guess. But like, do you have any pamphlets or flyers or whatever that I can take with me? You know, to drop in his mailbox and see if he mentions it in conversation that he's been recently."

Todd's suspicious look remained. He pointed to the corner by the double doors where there was a spinning display of pamphlets. "Over there."

Darn! Ali had wanted him to have to leave his desk.

She wandered over to the stand and began idly looking at the flyers, keeping one eye on Todd. He, meanwhile, was keeping an eye on her. She rotated the squeaky display, trying to get herself a bit more cover.

Just then, a beeping sound came from the desk. It sounded like some kind of alarm. Todd glanced up at the screen behind him, then fumbled to unclip the walkie-talkie at his hip.

"Everything okay?" he said into it, sounding panicked.

Through a gap in the flyers, Ali observed silently. On the screen she saw a bunch of kids had gotten into a shoving match. A female staff member in the same uniform as Todd was attempting to break them up, while shouting animatedly into her walkie-talkie.

"You're going to have to handle it," Todd said, looking harried. "I have to supervise the desk."

His gaze went to Ali, half hidden behind the pamphlet display. Ali realized this was her moment. She took one of the pamphlets and waved it in the air at Todd.

"Found it!" she announced.

She pushed through the glass doors and out onto the sidewalk. She waited, peeking through the glass as Todd disappeared back through the white doors she'd first seen him enter.

Ali hurried back inside.

On the security screen she could now see both Todd and his colleague grappling with the fighting kids. She didn't know how long she'd have, so she quickly launched herself onto the reception desk, stomach first, legs dangling behind her, and snatched up the sign-in book. She quickly flicked through the pages to find the date of Preston's murder, then scanned all the names listed.

There it was, in plain blue ink: *O'Neal + 3.*

So Kerrigan had been telling the truth. His alibi checked out. He wasn't the killer.

Ali lay supine across the reception desk, staring at the name in the book, her heart sinking at the realization that her investigation had already hit a dead end.

"Hey!" she heard an angry voice snap.

Ali dropped the book and slid off the desk, landing awkwardly on her feet. She turned to see Todd emerging through the industrial doors with two pissed off boys held in each of his hands by the collars of their shirts.

"Thanks! Bye!" she exclaimed.

She hurried away, out into the bright seaside sunshine.

This couldn't be the end, Ali knew. There were plenty of people in this town who could have done it. She would just have to go back to where it all went down, she realized with a shiver—back to the pier…

*

It took a while for Ali's heartbeat to return to normal. The run-in with Todd had been a close call, though somewhat exhilarating, if she were honest. Not that she would've enjoyed the experience quite so much if Todd had been a beefy six-foot-something security guard rather than a pimply high school graduate...

She headed for the boardwalk, mulling over everything she'd learned that morning about Preston. It seemed like everyone thought he was an odd guy. An annoyance. Was she barking up the wrong tree with this whole enemies theory? Was it more likely that the balloon man was the innocent victim of bullies?

She looked around. Everyone who passed looked suddenly suspicious. Ali had no idea where she was going to find her next lead...

"Ali!" a voice called.

She halted. Nate was trotting toward her, in boardshorts and nothing more. In the bright sunshine, his torso looked golden.

"Nate?" she said, her mouth going immediately dry. "How are you?"

"Me? I'm fine," he said. "It's you I'm worried about." Concern flashed in his eyes.

"Why are you worried about me?" Ali asked, scratching her neck. Having his focus so intently on her was making her quite hot under the collar.

Nate's eyes sparked. "Well, because you saw the body!"

"Oh. That."

Ali had been so distracted by Nate's hotness, she'd briefly forgotten all about her woes. They came crashing back down around her in an instant.

"Who told you that?" she asked.

"Delaney," Nate replied. "So it's true? You were there when he was reeled in?"

He sounded genuinely concerned for her well-being. She could add him to the list of people in this town who didn't have it in for her. A list easily counted on one hand.

"I was there," Ali told him. "But I'm doing fine."

He reached out and touched her arm. Ali's skin prickled.

"Are you sure?" he pressed. "Because if you're not fine, that's totally normal. I know I'd be a blubbering wreck if he'd died the same night he'd accosted me."

Ali could hardly tear her eyes off his golden-hued hand resting on her fish-belly-pale arm.

"I'm sure," she squeaked. "Thanks for checking."

Nate removed his hand. Without the distraction, Ali's brain finally reengaged.

"Wait," she said, looking at him questioningly. "He accosted you?"

Nate shrugged like it was no big deal. "Sure. I mean, every new store owner gets the Preston Lockley treatment. He comes in, shouts at us and threatens to ruin us, yadda yadda. If he'd gone on to be murdered the same day he'd done that to me, I'd be a gibbering paranoid wreck about it. 'Cause, you know... it gives you a motive."

Ali knew all too well it gave her a motive. Only by what Nate was telling her, it sounded like a motive shared by more store owners along the boardwalk than just hers. As his revelation sank in, Ali realized that Kerrigan's situation with Preston was far from unique. It wasn't just her store he was hassling for the lease of, it was everyone's.

She became suddenly animated.

"Which other stores got the 'Preston Lockley treatment'?" she questioned Nate. "Specifically."

He looked surprised by the 180 in her demeanor. "I only know of the ones that opened up after me."

"Which ones were they?" Ali pressed.

Nate's eyes widened further. "Since I moved here? Er, well, the book shop." He pointed it out. "And the bikini store."

"Great!" Ali said, suddenly energized. "I'll see you around, okay?" She turned and headed toward the bookstore.

"Oh. Yeah. Okay," she heard Nate say from behind her. "And if you need to talk, you know where I am."

"Thanks!"

She flashed two thumbs up over her shoulder and hurried away, leaving Nate standing alone and confused on the boardwalk.

CHAPTER TWENTY

Of all the brightly colored stores on the boardwalk, Bookworms was the brightest of them all. Its facade was painted every color of the rainbow, which appealed to Ali's inner child. If only she was visiting under better circumstances...

Inside, the decor was just as bright. The walls were blue, and all the signs were painted onto wooden white clouds, to make it look like the sky. The rows of wooden bookshelves were lacquered to show off the grain, and had big green leafy plants in pots on top of them, making a strange sort of forest. All the stools and chairs for reading were shaped like flowers or painted to look like mushrooms. A huge rainbow arched across the entire store, going up onto the ceiling before ending at a big golden pot with a leprechaun statue next to it. His speech bubble proclaimed: *Donate your change to help send books to the world's poorest children.* It was, quite simply, the most charming place Ali had ever been.

The store was cordoned off into separate reading nooks, each decorated with a different theme. Ali glanced around, looking for the clerk. She found her in an underwater-themed area, with shimmering decorations dangling from the ceiling and a big squishy octopus bean bag to sit on. She was a young woman, petite, with light brown hair cut into a pixie crop. She was wearing a relaxed pair of jeans, ripped at the knees, and a bright pink vintage T-shirt. A pair of battered Converse shoes completed the look.

Her appearance didn't exactly scream murderer. In fact, she reminded Ali of her thirteen-year-old self. She'd had a penchant for Converse as a teen.

"Ooh, hello," the clerk said, tunefully, when she noticed someone was there. She stood, placing the handful of books she'd been sorting onto the shelf. "Do you need any help?"

Ali noticed her name tag. Jenna.

"I do," she said. "But it's not literary related."

"Oh?" Jenna asked.

"I just opened a new store along the boardwalk," Ali explained. "I'm offering free coffee to all the local businesses, as a sort of hello neighbor." She was quietly proud of how quickly she'd managed to think of that on her feet. Teddy would be impressed by how much her improvisation skills were improving. "This place is incredible, by the way," she added.

Jenna smiled sweetly. Despite her childlike features, the crow's feet beside her eyes indicated she was actually older than her fashion choices might suggest.

"Well, thanks, new neighbor," she said with an inviting chuckle. "Kids love rainbows. And I just so happen to love coffee. I'll definitely be taking you up on your offer. Which one is your store?"

"Seaside Sweets," Ali said.

The change in Jenna was instant. The big grin faded from her face. Her eyes bulged with alarm. It didn't take a genius to work out why. She'd heard the rumors about Ali, and thought she was standing face to face with a killer.

It didn't matter that Ali was entirely innocent; her stomach still dropped with shame.

"You've heard of me, huh?" she asked, sadly.

Jenna turned to the shelf and started neatening the books, busying herself with an unnecessary task so as to avoid eye contact.

"I'm not sure if I have," she murmured in response, lying incredibly unconvincingly.

"No?" Ali replied. "I'm right by the pier. Sandwiched between Emilio's and Marco's pizzerias."

Jenna could pretend she'd not heard the rumors about Killer Ali from the Bakery, but there was no way she could pretend not to know the suave Italian twins.

"Oh... yes, maybe I do know it," Jenna said, evasively.

Her voice seemed to have gone up in pitch by about an octave. She was no longer able to meet Ali's eyes.

Ali felt awful that her mere presence could cause such discomfort in another, and it didn't do much for her self-esteem to be treated like some kind of dangerous animal. She very much wanted to get out of Bookworms as quickly as possible. But she still had to find out if what Nate had told her about Preston hassling all the new store owners was true, and whether Jenna had an alibi for the night of his murder. As much as it made Ali squirm, she'd have to cut right to the chase.

She drummed her fingers on the top of the brown wooden bookshelf. "You heard about what happened on the beach, I take it?"

"With the dead man?" Jenna replied, reticently. "Yes, of course."

"Did you know him? His name was Preston Lockley. I understand he was pretty well known in these parts."

Jenna seemed to be shrinking before Ali's eyes.

"Of—of course," she stammered. "Everyone did. I met him the day I opened my store. He came in here and…" She mumbled herself to silence.

"…And?" Ali pressed.

Jenna's eyes went big and round. She shook her head, clearly not wanting to finish her sentence.

"…And accused you of stealing his lease from under his nose?" Ali offered for her.

A frown flitted across Jenna's forehead. "How did you know that?"

"Because he did the same to me," Ali explained. "And a bunch of others, apparently."

So Nate was right. Preston had had a habit of hassling the stores along the boardwalk. It wasn't just her he'd argued with, she just happened to be the person he'd argued with before his death.

"Oh. Well." Jenna shrugged, dismissively. "There you go."

She was giving off very clear *leave me the hell alone* vibes, and Ali couldn't blame her. As far as Jenna was concerned, she was conversing with a potential killer. But the fact she even thought that was reason enough for Ali to ignore her very clear non-verbal signals. Despite how awkward and uncomfortable it made her feel, it was better to have a few awkward social interactions now, rather than spend the rest of her life having them in prison.

"Seems like we all have that in common," Ali added, trying to prove to the terrified woman they were on the same side. "Scary to think there's a killer out there. I know I won't be going for lonely strolls on the pier at night again anytime soon. One close call is enough for me." She felt beyond awkward at her clumsy attempt to steer the conversation in the direction she needed. She drummed her fingertips self-consciously on the shelf. "You?"

"What about me?" Jenna asked.

"Did you have a close call on the pier that night?"

Okay, this was getting ridiculous. Ali was being so far from subtle with her question she may as well have out and out asked Jenna if she had an alibi. As it stood, she didn't need to. Jenna was smart enough to read between the lines.

"Are you asking me if I have an alibi?" the young woman asked, looking both incredulous and afraid at the same time.

"No!" Ali exclaimed, trying to think of a way to backtrack out of this dead end she'd steered herself into. "I'm just, I dunno, just really freaked out and building up a picture is my coping strategy."

Jenna's face softened, but her eyes remained suspicious.

"I didn't see him that day," she said. "Or that evening. I closed up at the usual time and went home to watch TV with my housemate." She folded her arms with finality. "If that's not enough for you and you want to do some research on me, the show is an epic fantasy and that night the main dragon died."

Ali's questions had infuriated her. If she could be that annoyed just by being asked a question, you might think she'd be able to empathize with Ali and the difficult situation she'd found herself in.

But it wasn't to be. Instead, she glowered at Ali, seething, blowing air through her nostrils much like a dragon in her epic fantasy.

"Thanks," Ali mumbled.

She hurried out the bookstore and back onto the boardwalk, her heart racing. The whole encounter left her cheeks burning. And being covert clearly wasn't going to work. Everyone already knew who she was and had tarnished her with the murderer label. She'd have to try a different approach in the next store.

Boardwalk Bikinis was, somewhat amusingly to Ali, positioned directly next to Bookworms. She went inside, a blast of air conditioning cooling the nervous sweat on her neck and palms.

She glanced around, her eyes catching the amazing stock of bikinis. In other circumstances, she'd love to buy one. But she couldn't splurge on luxuries anymore, not with her business in such a perilous situation. In fact, she may never be able to have luxuries again if she didn't solve this murder. Prison commissaries didn't exactly stock fashionable beachwear.

"Can I help you?" a voice said.

Ali turned to face the bikini store owner. She was the typical California beauty, wearing Daisy Dukes that showed off endlessly long, tanned legs and bleached blonde hair. She looked like the sort of girl Ali would expect to see on Nate's arm, and she found herself inexplicably struck by a pang of jealousy. She swiftly brushed it aside. There were more pressing matters at hand than her hormones.

"Hi!" Ali said, brightly. "I'm new in the neighborhood and just wanted to check out the stores."

She dropped the whole free coffee thing. What was the point? Even coffee-lover Jenna had backtracked when she'd found out who Ali really was.

"Oh, cool. Willow Bay is a great place to live. How are you finding it?"

"Honestly, not what I was expecting," Ali said. "I mean, a dead body washed up on the beach pretty much after I arrived so…"

"OMG!" the girl cried, her eyes widening with excitement. "That is literally the craziest thing to ever happen here. The guy was like the local perv as well. He was always in here 'looking' at the bikinis, if you know what I mean."

Bikini Woman was a gossiper. Ali knew her exact type from high school. All you had to do with them was plant the seed and sit back and let them talk the rest.

"I've heard that from some other people too," Ali said. "The woman next door said he'd hassled her over her lease?"

The girl rolled her eyes. "Same. Such a freak. Weirdos like him will come up with any excuse to stare at girls."

Ali didn't mention the fact that Preston genuinely only came in because he wanted the store.

"So he came in here a lot?" she pressed.

"At first," Bikini Woman replied, shrugging her golden-tanned shoulders. "Like the first week I opened, maybe. But after I told my landlord about it, he stopped. Next thing I know, he washes up dead on the beach." She leaned closer to Ali and whispered conspiratorially. "I heard it was the new store owner who killed him. I'm not surprised. There are some people whose buttons you just don't want to push."

Ali hoped she could get out of here before Bikini Woman realized *she* was the subject of the rumors.

"Did you hear he was pushed off the pier?" Ali prompted.

"Yes. Like OMG. Can you even imagine?" The woman mimed pushing someone. "You'd have to be so big to push a fully grown man over the railings, right? Big or mad." She chuckled. "Or both."

It was a good point. Bikini Woman didn't have any visible muscles on her thin frame. The only way she was pushing anyone off the pier was if she head-butted them like a bull with a run up. Which seemed highly implausible to Ali…

"I was literally on the pier on the night he was pushed," Ali told her.

"Shut up! No way!" the girl cried, grabbing her arm tightly in her tanned hand. "That is totally scary. I'm so glad I was at home at the time. I was supposed to be on a date, but he canceled like ten minutes before, so I just watched TV and ate like, a kilo of frozen yogurt." She patted her non-existent belly fat.

"Was it the dragon show?" Ali asked.

"Yes!" the girl squealed with delight. "Do you watch it, too?"

"Oh yeah," Ali lied. "The last episode was a real tearjerker."

Bikini Woman pressed a hand to her heart and pouted exaggeratedly. "I know, right. Poor Raquel."

Raquel? Ali thought. *The dragon was called Raquel? What kind of stupid show was this?*

This was useless. Unless Bikini Woman and Jenna from Bookworms had colluded, neither of them had anything to do with Preston's killing.

But something Bikini Woman had said had piqued her curiosity.

"You said your landlord spoke to Preston for you. To scare him off?"

The woman nodded. "He was pretty angry about it. He said the same thing happened when he opened up his pizzeria, that Preston wouldn't leave him alone."

"Pizzeria?" Ali repeated. "Your landlord isn't one of the Italian twins, is it?"

"No, no, no," Bikini Woman said with a laugh. "My landlord's Fat Tony. He owns a bunch of restaurants and pizzerias in Willow Bay. Actually, I think my store is the only one of his that doesn't sell food."

She laughed and tossed her golden hair over her shoulder, as if completely oblivious to the very obvious reasons someone might break their own rules to lease a store to someone like her.

"Your landlord is called Fat Tony?" Ali repeated, raising an eyebrow.

The woman laughed. "I know. Sounds like he's in the mafia. But he's a gentle giant really. After I spoke to him about Preston, the guy never came in to hassle me again. Plus, he gets pizza and cannoli delivered to me from his restaurant for lunch. For free! Not exactly the actions of a mafioso…"

Ali found the conversation very illuminating. It seemed the two other new store owners in Willow Bay had indeed received the

"Preston Lockley treatment." But that didn't get her any closer to solving his murder.

Ali decided that Fat Tony was the next person she should speak to. But despite Bikini Woman's assurance he was a gentle giant, Ali didn't feel particularly enthused about seeking him out. He sounded like trouble to Ali.

Suddenly, Ali's grumbling stomach reminded her it was lunch time. She had to get back to the store to open it up in case of any lunch customers. Her search for Fat Tony would have to wait.

CHAPTER TWENTY ONE

Ali hurried to the bakery. When she made it back, she discovered Marco and Emilio outside their respective pizzerias, having a very animated argument across her storefront.

"Of course it's not a coincidence!" Marco was screeching. "There is no way you thought of fennel sausage topping 'coincidentally' at the same time I thought of fennel sausage topping! You stole my idea!"

"Because the concept of sausage on pizza is *so unique* I couldn't possibly have thought of it independently to you?" Emilio yelled in response.

Ali approached cautiously, looking back and forth from one handsome, angry Italian twin to the other.

"Guys... what's going in?" she asked.

Emilio put his hands on his hips. "Marco is accusing me of *copying* his idea for a topping!"

"It was the NEXT DAY!" Marco screamed, adopting the exact same posture as his brother. "You saw my sign advertising it, and the next thing I know you're, selling it too!" He looked at Ali and reiterated, "The NEXT DAY!"

Ali held her hands up in truce. If it hadn't been for the murder investigation hanging over her head, she might've found this amusing. But right now, it was the last thing she needed.

"I don't want to get in the middle of warring brothers," she said, though the romance books on her shelves suggested otherwise. "And do you think you guys might be able to keep it down? I know people aren't exactly clamoring to buy my butterscotch beignets, but you two shouting across my door isn't going to help matters."

To Ali's surprise, the brothers immediately ceased. She was so used to being the youngest of three siblings that getting her own way was a novelty.

"Your store is neutral territory," Marco said.

"No-Man's-Land," Emilio added, quickly.

"The demilitarized zone," Marco bounced back, frowning at him.

"Switzerland," Emilio hissed, his matching dark brows furrowing.

Ali rolled her eyes. So much for getting her own way.

"I just asked you not to argue in front of my store," she said, "and now you're arguing over who can come up with a better name for the truce?"

"Sorry," Emilio said sheepishly.

"Sorry," Marco mumbled.

Ali wasn't sure why they'd so quickly deferred to her request, but she was grateful all the same. She really could do without two warring people either side of her, to add to all the other crap she was dealing with.

"Hey, did you guys know Preston? It seems like he pestered just about every store owner on the boardwalk. What about you?"

"No," they said in unison, hurrying to be the one who spoke first.

"I opened my pizzeria before he started coming around," Emilio said.

"As did I," Marco added. "I opened my store before even Emilio."

"That's not true," Emilio contested. "I opened my pizzeria in May, and yours was in June."

"But I got the property first," Marco replied. "I just took my time decorating, unlike you."

"Speaking of your pizzerias," Ali said loudly, drowning out their petty bickering and steering the conversation back to the issue at hand. "Do either of you lease your stores from Fat Tony?"

"No," they said in matching horror.

"We would never do business with a man like him," Emilio said.

"He's bad news," Marco added.

This, it seemed, was something they could agree on.

"Anyway, ours are family businesses," Emilio explained. "Inherited."

"Well, *mine* is," Marco interjected. "They had to buy Emilio his store because he refused to share."

"I didn't refuse to share!" Emilio cried. "You were the one who said the store should be yours!"

"Because I'm older!"

"By two minutes!"

They descended into another argument. Ali was getting nowhere with the two of them. She headed inside her bakery. She needed a strong coffee after the morning she'd had.

She hadn't made it to the counter before the sound of the bell over the door interrupted her. She swirled around, excited for the briefest second that she may have a customer. But it was just Teddy.

Just Teddy? What was she thinking? It was Teddy! Her favorite person!

She ran to him.

"Teddy-bear," she cried, clinging to him like he was a life raft and she was adrift in the ocean. "I am so glad to see you!"

"And I'm so glad you're not dead," Teddy replied.

Ali let go and peered up into his eyes. "You heard about the murder?"

Teddy looked at her sternly. "Yes. I heard about the murder. Why the heck didn't you tell me?"

"It's all been a bit of a blur, to be honest," Ali said, meekly. "I can't remember who I have and haven't spoken to about it all."

Teddy did not look convinced.

"I promise," Ali insisted. "Seeing a dead body screws with your head a bit."

Her brother's eyes bulged. "You SAW the BODY? Okay. Get me a coffee and a croissant. We need to talk."

Ali obliged, and they sat in the window seat with steaming mugs of coffee and baked goods.

"I came here straight from an audition," Teddy told her. "I saw the story on the news that a body had washed up on the beach at Willow Bay and almost had a heart attack. I thought it might've been you. That your first day without customers had gone so badly you'd thrown yourself off the pier."

"Teddy!" Ali exclaimed, smacking his arm. "That's not funny. Don't joke about that sort of thing."

"I'm not joking," Teddy said firmly. "You know what Hannah's like when she spirals. She gets all secretive and stops letting people in. I don't want you to do that when things get hard, okay? You know I've always got your back. You just have to keep me in the loop."

He sounded like her father. Or what Ali imagined her father would sound like if he was still in her life to give her stern admonishments-cum-pep-talks.

"Fine," Ali said. "You want the loop. Here's the loop. Preston Lockley, a forty-year-old man who lived with his mother and was obsessed with balloons, washed up dead on the beach with a big blow to his head. The cops suspect foul play. He was obsessed with opening

111

his own balloon store on the boardwalk, so harassed everyone who opened a new store. The police suspect one of the newbies was the perp, and since I'm the only one who doesn't have an alibi and stupidly placed herself at the scene of the crime, I'm the one they're focusing on."

Teddy looked horrified. "Oh, Ali-cat. What a mess."

"I guess you could call it that," Ali said glumly.

Teddy tapped his chin as he pondered. "We need to think out of the box. Who would want to kill him? Did he have a maid? A butler? You know, some kind of disgruntled staff member who wanted his money?"

Ali rolled her eyes. "Teddy. You're just listing telenovela tropes. This is real life. No one has *butlers* anymore."

"They're tropes for a reason, Ali-cat. Because the most obvious suspect is usually the correct one. So. Was he rich?"

Ali thought of the shabby decor in the Lockley's household. "Nope. I mean, the houses up on the hill are obviously a little fancier than the little cottages down here, but I'd hazard a guess that maids aren't in their budget. Nurses, yes. Maids, no."

"Nurses?" Teddy queried.

"His mom has Alzheimer's. She has a visiting nurse."

Teddy raised his eyebrows with skepticism.

Ali considered the Asian nurse for a moment, recalling the diminutive woman sitting in her oversized green scrubs, her legs dangling over the couch edge as she munched on apple pie.

She shook her head. "No. It wasn't the nurse. She was way too small to push Preston off the pier."

Teddy munched thoughtfully on his croissant. "I assume he didn't have a wife, if he lived at home. But what about an ex? Lovers and former lovers are always the most likely suspect."

"His main passion in life was balloons," Ali said. "He spent his spare time making a Claymation documentary about the Hindenburg disaster. What do you think?"

Teddy shrugged a shoulder. "There's someone for everyone, Ali-cat."

She gave him a look.

"Okay," Teddy conceded. "So no ex-lover."

Ali slumped back in her seat, feeling defeated. "Let's just face it. The most obvious suspect is me."

"No," Teddy said firmly. "There has to be someone we're missing."

But Ali couldn't be cheered from her feeling of desolation.

"He was harassing me the night he died, and there are a whole load of witnesses," Ali said. "That gives me a really clear motive. I'm a new person who admitted to being on the pier the night he was killed. That gives me the opportunity."

"What about the means?" Teddy said, completing the triad with a hopeful tone.

Ali shook her head glumly. "The pier itself provided the means, doesn't it?"

Teddy's grin faded. "I guess that does look kind of suspicious."

"You're right," came a formidable voice from behind. "It does sound suspicious."

Ali gasped and turned. Standing in the open doorway was Detective Elton.

CHAPTER TWENTY TWO

Ali immediately felt panicked as Detective Elton paced inside the store. She leapt up from the window seat like she'd been caught doing something illegal, and hurried for the counter.

"Are you here for your free coffee?" she blathered as she took her place behind it.

But it was quite obvious from the detective's demeanor that she was not.

"No," Detective Elton said, darkly. "I'm here to ask you why you chose to omit from your statement the fact you argued with the victim the day before he was found dead on the beach." She pushed her sunglasses onto the top of her head and peered at Ali with suspicious eyes. "In our first conversation, you said you didn't know him."

"Because I didn't," Ali said weakly. "I had only met him that one time. If you'd asked me if I'd *met* him before, I would've said yes. But at the time he washed up on the beach, I didn't even know his name."

"Ah. It's an issue with semantics," Detective Elton said through her tightened jaw. "Let me say this as clearly and precisely as I can. CCTV cameras show you at the entrance of the pier going in, and not coming out again for a fairly substantial amount of time. A period of time that just so happens fits with our pathologist's time of death."

Ali swallowed the lump in her throat. How could she explain what she'd been doing that night in a way that would satisfy the detective? Staring at the ocean and thinking of her missing father hadn't gone down particularly well last time…

"I was taking a long stroll," Ali said. "Unwinding after a long day at work. It was my opening day, you see, and it hadn't gone as well as I'd hoped it would." Her chest sank with disappointment all over again at the disaster her first day had truly been.

"That's interesting," Detective Elton said, leadingly. "Have you always taken long strolls alone to unwind from your day at work?"

Ali frowned. She couldn't tell where this was going but she had a suspicion it wasn't anywhere good.

She shrugged. "No, not really. I had a boyfriend to vent to back then."

Detective Elton nodded once. "I see. That's a shame. Perhaps if you'd gone for one of your meditative evening strolls instead you wouldn't have been fired for assaulting a customer."

Ali's eyes widened with alarm. How the heck did the cops know about her crème brûlée smooshing antics? They must've contacted her old boss, Russell, for a character statement. Which meant she was pretty high up their list of suspects.

Ali pictured Russell reveling in that phone call, relaying what a terrible employee she'd been to Detective Elton, reinterpreting the crème brûlée smooshing incident as an assault. Her heartbeat accelerated, fast enough for her to hear the whooshing in her ears.

Teddy leapt up from the window seat and hurried to her aid.

"That was her one discretion," he told Detective Elton. "Ali's a saint."

The female detective peered at him. "Who are you?"

"I'm her brother," Teddy said confidently. He offered his hand for her to shake. "Teddy."

Detective Elton looked at his proffered hand, then back up at Teddy. "Teddy Sweet? What was wrong with your parents?"

Teddy's mouth opened with offense. He let his hand fall back to his side.

Detective Elton looked back at Ali. She smiled without emotion. "It won't be long before we learn just how saintlike Ms. Sweet really is. You may put up such an innocent front but I for one don't trust you. You may have Callihan and the rest of the men fooled, but you can't fool me."

She turned and headed for the door, but paused and turned back at the threshold.

"One last thing," she said.

Ali gulped. "Yes?"

"How much are those cannoli? The pistachio-flavored ones?"

Ali blinked in surprise. "Two dollars each. Or two for three dollars."

Detective Elton let a beat pass, nodded, and marched out the door.

The moment it shut, Ali fell forward onto the countertop, deflating like a balloon, and buried her face in her arms.

Teddy came around the back of the counter and rubbed her back supportively. "That detective was a horrible human. Although, was it just me or did it sound like she secretly wants to buy your cannoli?"

Ali smacked him. "Teddy. Stop joking around. Didn't you hear what she said? She called Russell. About me. And he happily divulged to them that I'm violent. Add that to the CCTV footage of me lingering for too long on the pier, and I'm utterly screwed."

"No you're not," Teddy said, taking her by the shoulders reassuringly. "If you really were such a suspect, that interview would've taken place down at the station, not here in your store."

Ali chewed her lip. Maybe he was right. Detective Elton may just be trying to pressure her. To turn the heat up and get her to crack. If they had any concrete and substantial reason to accuse her, she'd be in an interrogation room right now.

Teddy gave her a kind smile. "You know the truth always comes out sooner or later."

"Then it had better be sooner," Ali said. "Because I don't have the luxury of later." Her gaze flicked to the retreating black-clad figure of Detective Elton. "They're closing their net in on me."

CHAPTER TWENTY THREE

Teddy left Ali to another day of zero customers. Well, one customer if she counted Teddy, but since he hadn't paid for his coffee or croissants, she decided not to.

She couldn't help her feelings of despair. Had this whole thing been a terrible mistake? The bakery? The move? Everything?

Ali needed to clear her head.

She headed out into the warm evening, locking the store behind her, and bumped straight into Scruff the stray dog.

"Hi, little guy," she said to him, crouching down and scratching him behind the ear.

He was living up to his name today, looking scruffier than ever.

"I don't have any leftovers for you," she told him.

Scruff tipped his head as if listening intently to her.

"I forgot to bag them up."

Forgot? Ali thought. *More like couldn't be bothered.*

She'd grown tired of the ritual of baking exceptional treats only to throw everything away at the end of the day.

"Sorry," she added, before turning and walking away.

Scruff trotted along beside her.

"Dude," Ali said. "I already told you. I don't have any food."

Marco had been right. Once you fed the dog, he'd never leave you alone. Which was fine by Ali; she could use the company.

With Scruff in tow, Ali passed the entrance to the pier and glanced over at Lavinia's caravan. Django the macaque monkey was sitting on the steps in his red satin waistcoat, sifting through the contents of a leather wallet. Ali glowered at him, recalling the moment he'd stolen her ten-dollar bill.

The memory felt like it was from a million years ago. That was from before she decided to move to Willow Bay. Before she'd opened her store. Before she'd embarked on this whole adventure.

Misadventure, more like, Ali thought with disappointment.

Just then, she spotted a man storming out of Lavinia's caravan, stomping hurriedly down the steps.

"You're a fraud!" he screamed as he went. "Your advice was terrible! My wife and my girlfriend both left me!"

"Uh-oh. Looks like Lavinia has another unhappy customer," Ali told the dog, who was watching the scene with an expression of curiosity.

As the angry man stormed past her, Scruff jumped back and growled.

"Hey, it's not his fault," Ali said, crouching so she and the dog were face level. "He's mad because Lavinia got under his skin and made him make a decision he regretted. Like me..."

It had been Lavinia's stupid recipe metaphor that had made her think about opening the store.

Scruff licked her nose. Ali blinked, surprised, and let out a small giggle. She hadn't realized just how much she needed to vent until that soppy dog had looked at her with those big, loving brown eyes.

"I mean, she made me think I could make my bakery a success," Ali continued. "Me! The crème brûlée girl." Her voice lowered as she became overwhelmed by sorrow. "It's so obvious it would fail. All I had to do was ask a handful of people if they ate carbs and I'd have known my dream was stupid."

Scruff yipped. Of course, Ali had no idea what the yip meant. It could've been a yip of "Yeah, ya dumb blond, what were ya thinking?" But it just as easily could've been a yip of "I'm still hungry, can we skip to the snack bit?" Or, as Ali decided, because it was what she needed the most right now, his yip meant, "I'm so sorry your dream didn't work out."

"Thanks, Scruff," she said.

She picked herself up off the ground and walked the length of the boardwalk until she came to Kookies, Miriyam's bakery. Unlike Seaside Sweets, Kookies had suffered no drop in customers since Preston's gruesome killing. If anything, it was busier than ever.

Ali watched the pair of teens at the counter point to the chalkboard behind Miriyam. They were selecting the new Killer Kookie.

Ali realized that far from putting people off, the crass advertising gimmick was drawing them in!

Miriyam handed two bright red cookies over the counter, and the teens exited. They giggled as they hurried past Ali, and she got a clear view of the frosted design on the front: a smiley face with X's for eyes.

Ali grimaced. What kind of a person would try to profit off a local disaster like that? What kind of psychopathic monster did it take to even come up with that idea in the first place?

Ali halted. Maybe the same psychopathic monster who'd committed the crime?

She mulled it over in her mind. Miriyam was clearly threatened by a new bakery opening on the boardwalk, especially one in a way better location than her own; because who would buy a cookie from the end of the boardwalk if they'd already filled up on pastry desserts? Miriyam, like every other store owner on the boardwalk, would've known about Preston's penchant for pestering new store owners. Perhaps she'd known from personal experience that it wouldn't be long before he accosted Ali and made a huge public scene. What if Miriyam decided to use that as a cover? Perhaps she'd killed him knowing everyone would blame Ali for the crime. And what if this whole Killer Kookie thing was her way of goading her? Of rubbing it in her face?

There was only one way to know for sure. Ali would have to confront her.

She looked down at Scruff. "I'm sure you've got better things to do with your time then help me, but if you do stick around, I promise you I'll get you a big bone to say thank you. Deal? Okay."

And with that, she went inside.

*

Of all the things Ali had done so far to try and solve Preston's murder, this one scared her the most. Miriyam intimidated her more than Detective Elton. At least Detective Elton had a code of ethics to live by. Miriyam was a loose cannon.

Miriyam glanced up from the counter as she approached. She gave Ali a saccharine smile.

"Sweetie," she said, her brown eyes narrowing with suspicion. "I see you've finally decided to come and taste some real food."

Ali narrowed her eyes in return. "It's Ali."

"What?" Miriyam asked.

"My name," Ali said thinly. "It's Ali."

Miriyam looked as if she couldn't care less what her name was. She looked at her dispassionately. "What do you want?"

Ali cut to the chase. "I wanted to try one of your new Killer Kookies," she said. "I hear they're 'to die for.'"

The fake smile appeared again on Miriam's lips. She folded her arms. "Too bad. I'm all out."

Ali peered over her shoulder. There were at least seven of the ghoulishly red cookies in the warming rack behind her ready to go.

"Really?" she asked.

Miriyam glanced over her shoulder, then back again. "Fine. I'll be honest. I don't want to sell to you. I don't trust you not to steal the recipe."

Ali was about to tell her the protégé of Milo Baptiste had zero need to steal someone else's recipe, but held her tongue. It seemed unwise to goad the woman. Particularly if she harbored a murderous instinct.

"I'm surprised they're proving so popular," Ali continued. "You'd think people would be put off by the color."

Miriyam shrugged. "I've given up trying to understand the tastes of Americans. It's not my job to judge."

Rich, Ali thought, feeling distinctly judged as an American.

"All I do is give the people what they want," Miriyam continued flippantly. "If they did not buy them, I would not make them. It's as simple as that. Supply. Demand." She used a lecturing tone, like she was teaching business studies 101 to a high schooler. "It's what makes my store thrive. Flexibility. Adaptability. Changing with the times. You wouldn't know that, because you make French desserts that no one's wanted to eat since the Victorian times."

Ali's eyebrows shot up. That was quite the tirade.

"Thanks for the advice," she said, tersely.

The bell over the door tinkled and Miriyam looked over Ali's shoulder. A cluster of pre-teens had entered and were now coagulating in a nervous clump behind her.

"Move along, please," Miriyam said, raising her voice over the noise of murmuring voices the kids had brought in with them. "These children behind you are what we successful business owners call 'customers.' You'd know that if you got any."

It took all of Ali's willpower not to blow a gasket.

Miriyam beckoned to the kids behind Ali, urging them to come closer. But Ali stood her ground, even as they jostled their way around her. She wasn't done yet.

"Where were you the night Preston died?" she demanded over several heads.

"Working," Miriyam replied simply, somehow managing to take their orders and carry on a conversation at the same time.

"*After* work," Ali added.

"There is no such thing as 'after work,'" came Miriyam's snooty reply. "When you are a serious businesswoman, you must work when the work presents itself."

Ali rolled her eyes. She'd had as much of the condescending lectures as she could stomach.

"So what, you were working your register all evening?"

Miriyam handed a sickly-looking cake on a stick across the counter to an eager, outstretched hand. "That sounds about right," she said. "It's what I do most evenings."

Just then, a couple of tubby boys elbowed their way past Ali, forcing her back a couple of paces. Ali had to raise her voice to call over the excited din of sugar addicts about to get their fix.

"You can corroborate that?" she pressed.

"To the police, yes," Miriyam replied. "Not to you. I owe you no explanations."

The bell tinkled again, and yet more pre-teens pushed their way into the store. These ones were more boisterous than the first. They didn't even wait for Miriyam to give them the go-ahead to push past Ali, they just went right ahead and did it of their own accord.

Ali couldn't help but scoff at their rudeness. She would never have been allowed to behave that way as a kid! But none of them were actually being supervised, she realized, and everyone knew what happened to kids when left to govern themselves. Lord of the Flies.

"Hey!" a kid shouted. "That's mine!"

Ali turned to see two kids wrestling over a cookie.

"It's mine!" the second said. "I ordered the gooey chocolate brownie."

"That's dark chocolate caramel!" the first girl cried.

"No it's not!" the boy shot back with a disproportionate amount of venom.

As a mini war broke out in front of Ali, the bell rang and yet more kids came filing in. Now she was swimming in them, up to her armpits in them. It was time to vamoose.

She began wading toward the exit. Which was when a shrill scream erupted from the front of the store. Ali swirled to see none other than Scruff standing on the counter, shoving his nose into the display cookies.

He must've slid in unnoticed through the legs of the children as they'd entered. The sudden sight of his furry presence caused pandemonium to erupt in the store.

"NO ANIMALS!" Miriyam cried. "NO ANIMALS!"

Ali couldn't help but smirk. It was nice to see the horrible woman knocked off her high horse for once.

As she reached the door, Ali turned back and caught Scruff's eye. His jaws were stretched around a giant chocolate chip cookie. He leapt down from the counter, taking his stolen goods with him, and charged toward her, cleaving a path in the middle of the screeching children as he did.

Ali shut the door after him, cutting out the cacophony of noise, and watched with amusement at the utter pandemonium he'd caused inside.

CHAPTER TWENTY FOUR

Ali's moment of schadenfreude was short-lived, because she was no closer to solving the case, and not only was she the prime suspect, but she'd run out of leads to pursue.

She had her suspicions about Miriyam and her insensitive marketing gimmick, but she wasn't sure if that was really enough to go on. Dyeing a cookie red to mimic blood was very different from killing someone. And besides, Preston wasn't exactly a small guy. Ali doubted whether a woman would have the strength to throw a body from the pier, even one with baker's muscles.

Scruff yipped at her.

"You're right," she said. "I did tell you I'd buy you a bone for sticking around. Come on."

She led her furry companion as far as the closest convenience store, ducking inside to find the biggest and tastiest-looking dog treat in the pet aisle, and presenting it to Scruff.

"Thanks for all your help today," she told him.

Scruff looked like all his Christmases had come early. He snatched the bone from her hands and took off down the street at a clip. Ali felt a small pang of sadness that the fluffy critter had abandoned her the moment he'd gotten his snack.

She headed back to her store, which was now in darkness, and hit the lights as she entered.

She glanced around at the bakery—her dream that had turned into a nightmare.

If she shut down now, she might be able to avoid going into major debt. Of course Teddy's money was gone, and she'd have to find a way to pay him back, but she could resell the coffee machine and baking oven. Claw back a bit that way. And maybe she could sweet-talk Kerrigan out of paying any rent, since the store was in much better shape to rent out now than when she'd taken it. Which was more than could be said for her apartment. The little place had been woefully neglected during her time here. She hadn't even finished unpacking her boxes. Of course there was always the bail and run option, but Ali

123

could never be that cruel. Kerrigan was her landlord for the store and the apartment. Skipping on him would be unforgivably cruel.

Ali felt all-around terrible. So terrible she knew none of her usual cheer up routines would help. She needed to pull out all the stops...

It was cupcake time.

When Ali was a kid, she and her dad would make cupcakes as comfort food. In fact, it was this ritual that got Ali interested in baking in the first place. Over the years, she'd perfected the recipe and now could whip the delicious lemon coconut cupcakes from memory.

She went into the kitchen and fetched her dry ingredients—all-purpose flour, sugar, baking powder, and half a teaspoon of salt—sifting them into the bowl. Then she zested a lemon into the bowl with the dry ingredients and set it aside.

Next she moved on to the wet ingredients. She squeezed the lemon on a juicer and poured the juice into a new bowl before adding vegetable oil, buttermilk, and coconut milk. She turned on the beaters. Most people underbeat their cupcakes. Ali had learned one of the best tricks for perfect cupcakes was to beat them way longer than you'd expect. That, and adding the eggs one at a time, yolk first. And using real vanilla rather than extract.

She left the beaters to their thing, using a hand whisk to mix the egg whites and sugar until they made thick fluffy peaks. Then she added the wet and dry ingredients together under the beaters, threw in some shredded coconut and scraped vanilla, and left them to churn away.

As Ali added the shredded coconut, she thought wistfully of her father. Coconut had been his favorite ingredient. He'd always tried to sneak more into the batter, and it became a silly game, with Ali trying to stop him, or fetching her dolls to guard the bag of shredded coconut before he could steal it. The memory made her happy and sad all at once. She sprinkled in extra coconut in her father's honor.

As she measured the batter into the muffin cups with an ice cream scoop, she couldn't help the pang of grief she felt for her missing father. What she wouldn't give to have him here, offering advice and support in her difficult times.

She set the oven at 350 degrees and popped in the batch of cupcakes. All she had to do now was kill twenty minutes, and then she could eat her woes away.

But just as she retrieved the batch from the oven, the bell over the door tinkled. Ali frowned, not realizing she'd left it unlocked.

She headed from the kitchen to the main store. Standing in the bakery was a middle-aged man with a big wide grin.

"What *is* that amazing smell?" he asked, his blue eyes twinkling. He had a strange aura, like some kind of game show host, making "What *is* that amazing smell?" sound like his catchphrase.

"Lemon and coconut cupcakes," Ali told him, tentatively.

"Lemon and coconut cupcakes," he repeated, as if that were the most incredible combination he'd ever heard of.

Ali looked at him warily. She'd met her fair amount of oddballs working in LA but she'd never met a man quite as chipper as the one now standing in front of her. He gave off an old Hollywood vibe, like one of those gentle, suave, blue-eyed crooners her mom always put on at Christmas.

He tapped the counter decisively. "I'd like to buy a lemon and coconut cupcake."

Ali was surprised. She'd been dying for customers, and had failed to sell any of her amazing French desserts. But a cupcake? A simple cupcake?

"You—you want to buy a cupcake?" she stammered, her eyes scanning the gorgeous display of pastries that had failed to rouse any kind of interest in the man.

The man flashed her one of his game show host grins. "This is a bakery, isn't it?" he quipped.

"Well—well, yes. Yes, it is," Ali said. A shiver of excitement pealed through her. "Hold on one moment."

She hurried to the kitchen, adrenaline coursing through her, as she frantically attempted to work out how much she should charge for the cupcake. She'd just been making them for herself, so she could wallow in her misery; pricing had been far from her mind. And what about the frosting? She hadn't gotten around to frosting them yet. She couldn't sell them without frosting, surely?

She slipped on her oven gloves and grabbed the tray, which was still warm from the oven, and hurried back into the bakery.

When the man saw them, his eyes practically sparkled with delight. He sniffed the air deeply.

"I—I'm afraid I haven't frosted them yet," she said.

The man dismissed her concern with a flap of the hand. "If it tastes as good as it smells, I suspect it doesn't need frosting," he said.

Ali handed one across the counter to him. He took a bite and his eyes pinged wide open.

"That's incredible," he said through his mouthful, crumbs coating his top lip. "Better than incredible. That's phenomenal."

Ali didn't know how to react. Five minutes ago she'd been resigned to closing up shop forever and throwing all that training under Milo Baptiste out the window. Now there was a strange old-school Hollywood man standing in her bakery enthusing about the cupcake recipe she'd learned from her dad! Maybe it was a dream? Perhaps she'd dozed off in the kitchen and her semi-conscious brain had conjured up this moment? She pinched her arm just to be sure.

"Ow!"

Nope. Not a dream. The world's most positive man really was standing in front of her *mming* and *aahing* with every bite he took of the cupcake.

"How did you come up with such a creative cupcake?" the man asked through his mouthfuls.

"It's a family recipe," Ali told him. "I jazzed it up a bit over the years."

She'd actually jazzed it up *a lot* over the years, combining the skills she'd learned from Milo, as well as professional-grade equipment that hadn't been available back when she was a kid and had whisked the whole damn thing by hand.

"Well, it's hands down the best cupcake I've ever had in my life," Mr. Positive said with a grin. He clapped his hands, his cupcake now finished. "I'll take another."

Ali's eyes widened. "You want more?"

"I want more!" the man exclaimed.

Ali had never seen anyone look quite so excited by cupcakes. She started to question his sanity. But on the other hand, his positivity was infectious. He may well be a fruit loop, but Ali couldn't help herself. She smiled widely and handed a second cupcake across the counter to him.

He seemed to enjoy this one just as much as the first. The whole while he ate, he shook his head in a *hot damn* gesture.

"This place," he muttered happily under his breath before swirling out the door, pointing a finger at Ali, and exclaiming, "I'll remember this place!"

He strolled out, and Ali watched him go.

The bizarre encounter had lit a fire in her belly. It had given her a taste of the dream life she'd come here chasing. She knew her food was amazing, and she knew she could make Seaside Sweets a success, if she was given a fair chance.

But the only way she'd ever get that chance was if she solved Preston's murder and cleared her name.

Ali was ready to do anything. She was ready to throw herself into the investigation with fervor. It was time to reclaim her dream life.

CHAPTER TWENTY FIVE

Ali woke the next morning with a fire burning inside of her, and headed to her store to bake that morning's offerings. As she went, she glanced left and right across the buzzing boardwalk, determined to keep calling it her home.

When she reached her store, she spotted some perfectly formed dog poop right on the doorstep.

"Scruff," she muttered under her breath.

She hadn't seen her furry companion since she'd gifted him a jumbo bone. Clearly, that was all he wanted her for.

She headed inside, the smell of yesterday's coconut cupcakes still permeating the air, and set about making a selection of pastries on the off chance anyone popped in for breakfast. The selection she baked was growing smaller with every day that passed, not just because Ali knew no one would buy them, but because she was devoting more and more time to the murder investigation.

As predicted, no one came in to buy her breakfast croissants, and Ali locked up the store, heading out into the sunshine—carefully stepping over the poop—ready to begin another day of sleuthing.

Just then, movement made her jump. Someone was lurking behind the trash cans. Her heart went into her throat as she thought of Preston's murderer still on the loose, and feared she was the next victim on their hit list.

But instead of a knife-wielding maniac, a four-legged, furry creature slunk out toward her.

"Scruff!" Ali exclaimed. Relief swelled through every fiber of her being that she wasn't about to get bludgeoned to death. She crouched down and cupped his furry face in her hands. "You almost gave me a heart attack."

Instead of responding to her with his usual head tip or bark, Scruff let out the saddest whimper Ali had ever heard. It wasn't the sort of noise she'd heard him make when he wanted something; it was a whine of distress.

Ali's heart clenched.

"What's wrong, little dude?" she asked anxiously. "Are you okay? Sick? Hurt?"

Scruff whimpered again, even more loudly, and he let his head drop heavily into Ali's hands. His eyes looked glassy. His tongue lolled.

Ali started panicking. She didn't know what to do. She didn't know where any of Willow Bay's vets were. Even if she did manage to get Scruff to one, he was a stray. They'd impound him. Probably euthanize him. She couldn't let that happen. Her sleuthing would have to wait— saving Scruff's life was now her priority.

Ali sat down on the sidewalk and gently lowered the pup's head into her lap. He lay against the fabric of her blue jeans, whining softly.

With shaking hands, Ali retrieved her cell phone from her pocket, desperately racking her brains about who might be able to help her in this situation.

But before she got the chance, Scruff started making a horrible wheezing noise.

"Oh no!" Ali squealed. "Scruff! Scruff!"

Was the dog about to die in her arms?

Scruff's wheezing grew louder and raspier. His little body seemed to convulse in time with each gasp. Then suddenly, he threw up.

A huge pool of vomit splattered onto the sidewalk. Ali cried out and leapt out of the way just in time.

The dog looked up at her and wagged his tail. He appeared to be fully recovered from what Ali realized now had been retching, not convulsing.

"That was it?" Ali asked. "You just had to throw up!"

Scruff yipped at her happily and wagged his tail.

Ali was both disgusted and relieved. Scruff's vomit on the sidewalk was bright red, and Ali remembered the moment the naughty dog had raced inside and snatched a Killer Kookie right off of Miriyam's counter.

Ali folded her arms. "I think you've learned a very important lesson today," she told him. "Cookies aren't for dogs."

Scruff just ran merry circles round her legs.

The puddle of lurid vomit was right outside Ali's door, right next to the poop. She had some serious cleaning up to do if she didn't want to risk getting a health code violation to add on top of all her current woes.

She quickly headed inside the store and filled the mop bucket with warm water and disinfectant, then went back outside to wash away all the mess. Scruff watched on curiously, as his puddle disappeared into the guttering and down the drain.

Suddenly, Ali was struck by a thought. The poop's and vomit's potential to get her a health code violation had caused a lightbulb to go on in her head.

She swirled on the spot and stared at the front of Seaside Sweets. She tried to picture it as it had been back when it was the town's beloved pita store owned by Pete. Everyone raved about the place. It must've had tons of customers streaming in and out of its doors. So then *why* had it closed?

Kerrigan hadn't given her an explanation. All he'd said was that Pete's Pitas had closed down suddenly. So Pete's departure was totally unexpected. Completely out of the blue. Unimaginable even, given that Kerrigan was so confident in Pete continuing his lease forever that he'd even told Preston Lockley he'd be next in line for the store if it ever closed.

"Pete's Pitas didn't close voluntarily," Ali told Scruff, gasping with the sudden realization.

Scruff barked with excitement.

Ali finished her thought. "He was forced out!"

Her mind raced a mile a second as she mulled over her theory. There was only one reason Ali could think of that might cause someone to pack up and close up shop at a moment's notice, leaving their landlord in the lurch like that. Health inspectors.

With a surge of excitement, Ali fetched her cell phone and dialed Kerrigan. As the ring sounded in her ear, she peered up the hill at his canary-yellow house.

"Ali?" Kerrigan's Irish accent said into her ear.

"I have a question," Ali began, speaking to the yellow house. "About the store."

"Oh? Is anything wrong?"

"No, I mean it's about the store *before* I leased it. Back when it was Pete's Pitas."

A beat passed.

"Go on…" Kerrigan said, with a slightly wary tone.

"I'm wondering why it closed down in the first place," Ali said. "From everything I've heard—from you and all the locals—Pete's was a thriving business that was very well liked. You certainly weren't expecting him to pack up shop, were you?"

There was silence on the line.

Finally, Kerrigan said, "I was wondering when you were going to ask that."

He sounded nervous. Ali felt a sudden spark of intrigue in her chest. There was more to the story. She was right.

A warm breeze stirred the hairs at the back of her neck.

"Well?" she pressed.

"It was a health code violation," Kerrigan said through an exhalation.

"I knew it," Ali replied triumphantly.

"I'm so sorry," Kerrigan said. "I should've told you. It might be one of the reasons your store is struggling right now."

Ali paused, the celebration quickly ebbing out of her. "Wait. What?"

That hadn't been Ali's original intention for the phone call, but now the cat was out of the bag, she realized that, yes, Kerrigan should have told her the store had been closed down due to a health violation.

"They put big yellow and black hazard signs in the windows," he continued. "It's not the sort of image that fades particularly quickly from people's memories."

Ali's jaw clenched. Suddenly, the deal Teddy had managed to wrangle for her made a whole lot more sense. Kerrigan had rented her a property with a completely tarnished reputation. He must've been thrilled when an out-of-towner expressed interest in the place, because it meant he'd found someone who had no idea about the store's history.

Ali's mind went straight to black mold. Rats under the floorboards. Broken sewer pipes. She shuddered at the thoughts.

"What kind of health violation are we talking about here?" she demanded. "Is there something wrong with the property?"

"No, no, nothing like that," Kerrigan said. "It was tainted meat."

Ali grimaced. But at least it was a failing on Pete's part, rather than a problem with the store itself.

"That's gross," she offered.

Kerrigan continued. "Yes. It was gross. A bunch of people got sick. It was such a shock. Everyone trusted Pete so they felt so betrayed when it turned out he wasn't keeping up with health and safety protocols. He claimed it was a one-off but he knew no one would believe him, not after the posters had gone up in the window. He was forced to shut."

Ali's mind raced. Something didn't add up. Anyone who worked in food preparation knew the importance of hygiene. It was drilled into

131

them in culinary school, like how an army recruit is trained to make their bed perfectly every morning. Even if Pete hadn't gone the formal culinary school route, it still would've been drilled into him once he was on the job. For most chefs, proper hygienic practices were second nature. They knew all the intricacies of proper food storage and proper utensil cleaning. They knew the color-coded systems to ensure separate chopping boards were used for meats and vegetables, and to use separate dishcloths to clean the surfaces they'd touched, like the back of their hand. Ali could still recite the mnemonic she'd learned in school to remember it all by. It just didn't make sense to her that a thriving business owned by a beloved and trustworthy man would make such a mistake.

That's when Ali had her eureka moment.

Preston had engineered the tainted meat scandal to force Pete to shut his doors and leave the premises, thinking Kerrigan would keep his word and he'd finally get the lease for his balloon store. And perhaps Pete had worked it out and killed Preston in revenge.

Ali felt suddenly enthused to have a new theory to pursue.

"Does Pete still live in town?" she asked Kerrigan.

"Oh yes," her landlord replied. "He put so much work into that house of his, I doubt he'd ever be able to leave it. He probably couldn't, either. An Andy Warhol–style door isn't exactly the sort of thing that the general public wants."

Ali scanned the hillside for any doorways that resembled Andy Warhol's iconic bright pop art. She had some questions to ask the famous Pete of Pete's Pitas.

CHAPTER TWENTY SIX

Ali checked her watch. She was itching to put her plan into action.

Ten a.m. was a socially acceptable time to knock on a stranger's door and accuse him of murder, wasn't it? She decided yes. And on the slim chance anyone did choose to venture into the bakery for post-lunch sweets, they wouldn't do so until midday, which would give Ali a good two hours to try and squeeze a confession out of her new prime suspect...

She flipped the bakery's sign to *closed*, locked the door securely, and headed into the hills behind her store. She took the long main street that stretched up into the hills, passing Kerrigan's home on her way. As she followed the steeply inclined street upward, she scanned left and right at all the side roads, searching for an Andy Warhol–inspired front door.

Today, the California sunshine was unrelenting, and Ali puffed and panted beneath its powerful rays. As a jogger whizzed past her, she silently cursed herself for having such woefully weak leg muscles.

Once this is all over, I'm joining Irene's power-walking gang, she resolved.

She was a few hundred meters up the hill when the muscle pain grew too much, forcing her to stop. She bent forward, hands on knees, legs like jelly, unsure whether she could even take another step. A couple of stars started to dance in her eyes, and when she looked up, she realized she was seeing double. No, quadruple! Four Marilyn Monroes wavered in her vision.

Hold on a second, Ali thought.

She was seeing four Marilyn Monroes because she was outside the Andy Warhol door! Pete's house. She'd found it!

Ali straightened up with renewed vigor, pacing along the side street to get a better look. She stopped outside and scanned the building, waiting for her ragged breathing to even out.

Pete's house looked flamboyant; even amongst the brightly colored townhouses of Willow Bay it was the brightest. There were faux marble pillars either side of the door, and Gaudi-inspired glass tiles forming a wave design beneath one of the windows, adding a dash of Barcelona to the already eclectic mix of styles.

On first glance, it didn't seem like the sort of home a murderer would live in. But Ali reminded herself it was a fool's errand to try and apply logic to the bizarre mind of a calculated killer. Besides, there were plenty of murderers known for their meticulous taste. The grandeur could be a sign of a narcissistic personality.

With that chilling thought bouncing around her skull, Ali steeled herself and paced onto the doorstep. She rapped her knuckles against the door determinedly, right on Marilyn Monroe's pouty lips. Then she stepped back and waited, her heart slamming against her rib cage.

A moment later, the door opened. Standing before Ali was a very tall, very well-built man. A man who was easily big enough to overpower Preston and shove him off the pier. He was holding a golden Chihuahua in his arms and the dog had a fancy, diamond-encrusted collar around its neck.

"Yes?" the man asked, looking down his large nose at Ali.

Ali wanted to shrink away from him, but she held her ground. Her whole future in Willow Bay was on the line. If there was any time to be brave, it was now.

"Are you Pete?" she asked, sounding a thousand percent more confident than she felt.

"Yes," he confirmed.

By the look of his thinning dark hair streaked with silver, and slightly rubbery tanned skin, Ali guessed him to be in his fifties. And with his fancy house and pampered pedigree pooch, he clearly enjoyed a certain quality of life, one that may be proving difficult to maintain now his successful business had been stripped from him. His taste was clearly too expensive for the early retirement that had been forced upon him to be anything but a catastrophe.

Pete and his Chihuahua scanned Ali up and down with matching brown, beady eyes.

"Who are you?" Pete demanded.

"Ali Sweet," she replied brightly. "I lease your old store."

"Oh," he said. There was a shift in his demeanor. "Is anything amiss? Did I leave an outstanding bill or something?"

Ali shook her head. "No, no, nothing like that. I actually came here for advice."

Pete frowned. "Advice? What kind of advice?"

"Well, your store was very popular," Ali explained, keeping her tone as conversational as she could. "Which is more than I can say for my bakery. I've barely sold a thing. So I was hoping you might be able to teach me some tricks of the trade. Impart your wisdom on me."

She'd planned this whole thing out in advance. Her interview with Pete was going to start innocuously enough, before she veered into the murder situation, and finally hit him with the evidence she'd gathered against him: the tainted meat scandal that put a sudden end to his previously lucrative business, and stirred a murderous rage within him.

But first she had to butter him up. Psychopaths liked to be flattered. If she was even going to get her foot in the door to conduct her interrogation, she was going to have to fawn her way in.

Pete twisted his lips. "I guess I could give you some tips," he said. He widened the door for her to enter.

"You're a hero!" Ali exclaimed, with fake enthusiasm as she stepped inside.

The moment his back was turned, she let her grin drop.

As she followed him along the pristinely clean corridor, with its white walls, polished beech floorboards, and golden wall sconces, she thought again about just how large he really was. Easily large enough to tower over Preston and throw him from the pier.

"Do you want coffee?" Pete asked over his shoulder. "I've just brewed a pot."

"That sounds great," she said.

The corridor gave way to an enormous kitchen. Just like with Kerrigan's house, Ali was taken aback by the enormity of Pete's property on the hill.

Everything in the kitchen was state of the art. Shiny white-tiled floors and expensive black granite countertops. Skylights letting in the bright daylight. A huge double-doored fridge, with a separate wine fridge beside it. And the walls were decorated with Pete's Pitas posters, designed in an attractive retro style.

All signs point to narcissist... Ali thought. *And who cleans their house this spotlessly, if not a murderer?*

Every bit of Pete's kitchen was a beautiful feat of design, ordered, neat, and exquisitely decorated. Pete's Pitas must've been banking serious dollar in its heyday for him to afford all this.

But more importantly, Ali thought, Pete was a man who liked things to be clean. She couldn't picture him getting himself a health code violation. It must've been Preston's doing, she was sure of it.

135

"Take a seat," Pete said, gesturing to a trendy leather, shabby chic barstool at the black granite kitchen island.

Ali did, reminding herself not to get too comfortable or drop her guard. She could be in a killer's kitchen after all.

She watched Pete pace around the kitchen as he prepared the coffees, the whole while holding his Chihuahua in his arms like it was a baby being burped. The dog watched Ali in turn, its chin resting on Pete's shoulders, its round eyes bulging. As much as Ali loved all four-legged creatures, the tense energy coming from the neurotic-looking Chihuahua was putting her even more on edge. It was a bit like how she felt hanging out with Hannah, like they were constantly on the brink of disaster.

"Cute dog," she commented. "What's its name?"

"Tinkerbell," Pete said.

There was a stiffness in his tone, Ali noted. It was irrefutable. Her presence was making him uncomfortable, and not in the same way she'd made Jenna from Bookworms uncomfortable. It felt more like Pete was hiding something.

Her heartbeat accelerated. She wondered whether her hunch may well turn out to be correct. Had she really found Preston's killer?

"Do you want milk?" Pete asked, his back to her. "Cream? Sugar?"

"Black is fine," Ali replied, craning her head to see whether Pete was lacing her drink with poison or anything.

He came over and placed a steaming mug on the coaster in front of her. Ali could see no telltale signs of froth or residue, so decided it was safe. Still, she had no intention of drinking it. Instead, she grasped the mug in both hands, reasoning she could use the boiling coffee inside as a weapon if it came to it.

Pete took the stool next to her, spinning so they were facing one another.

Ali gulped. This was a little too close for comfort for her taste. She was close enough for the Chihuahua to lick her if it was so inclined, though since it looked utterly petrified of her, Ali guessed it wouldn't.

Pete rested his elbow on the granite counter and looked at her expectantly.

"So?" he asked.

Despite her racing heartbeat, Ali forced out a calm voice. "So I've heard a lot about how fantastic your store was. I'm wondering if you have any suggestions on how to replicate your success. I can't even get people through the door."

Pete's lips twisted. There was a slight tremble in them.

"No, I don't imagine it is easy for you to entice people inside," he murmured, his fingers playing with the edges of his coaster. "It's going to take a while before they're able to shake off the image of those—those awful hazard posters."

His voice cracked as he spoke. The memory was clearly still raw for him, and Ali was surprised by just how readily he'd brought up the scandal. She had not expected him to immediately admit to the health violation. Her carefully planned questions flew right out the window. Pete had skipped ahead, so she may as well just cut to the chase, as well.

"You were closed down because of a health violation, is that right?" she asked.

"Tainted meat," he said with a wistful sigh. "But I've no idea how it happened. I'd been doing that job for fifteen years. I wasn't complacent. I knew how to keep my kitchen hygienic."

"Do you think someone tampered with it?" Ali asked.

"I know someone did," Pete replied, emphatically. "Because it certainly wasn't me!"

"You must have some suspicions about who it was," Ali prodded.

Pete looked tense. "I assume it was a disgruntled ex-employee."

He said it with a distinct air of flippancy that Ali wasn't buying for a second. The man had lost his entire business. His entire livelihood. That wasn't something to be dismissive about. If the same thing happened to her, she'd do anything to find the culprit, come hell or high water.

"You must've been a scary boss," Ali said, chuckling in an attempt to play it off like friendly banter, "if you managed to instill such hatred in someone they got you shut down."

"You never can tell what resentments some people are harboring," Pete replied, thinly.

"Right..." Ali replied.

The atmosphere seemed to be growing frostier. Ali tightened her clasp on the mug, becoming increasingly concerned of the possibility she might need to throw her hot coffee in his face.

Her nerves seemed to rattle as she mustered every inch of confidence she could, and asked the crucial question. "Did you ever think that the culprit might have been Preston Lockley?"

Pete looked stunned. Too stunned. Too theatrical. It was like he knew she was going to bring Preston up and had rehearsed in his head how to act shocked. She knew this from Teddy. He'd practiced his shocked face on her about a million times. Over-hamming shock was one of the biggest pitfalls for an actor, in his opinion.

"Preston Lockley?" he repeated, with a gasp. "But he never even worked for me."

"He didn't have to be a past employee to have a grudge against you," Ali said.

Pete paused. His eyes narrowed. Ali's coffee cup started to quiver in her trembling hands.

"Why are you bringing a dead man into this?" Pete challenged.

"He wanted your store, didn't he?" Ali replied. "Isn't that reason enough to suspect he was the one who got you closed down?"

Pete's expression remained stony. He spoke through clenched teeth. "Preston was a nuisance, yes. But he had nothing to do with anything. It was a disgruntled employee. I'm certain of it."

She was getting to him now. He was rattled.

"How can you be so sure?" she pressed.

"I just am," he countered.

He seemed increasingly flustered. Ali knew that meant she was getting close. It was time to turn up the heat even more.

"Are you really telling me you never even considered Preston?" she continued. "The man had a history of screaming at store clerks. Who knows what else he did? He seemed like a loose cannon to me."

"No," Pete said simply.

"No, he wasn't a loose cannon, or no you never considered him?"

"I never considered him," he said firmly.

But Ali wasn't letting this go. She was clearly getting to him. Pete was rattled, and she just needed to give him the final push over the edge, much like how he pushed Preston into the ocean.

"But who was more disgruntled than Preston?" she pressed. "Who would actually go to the lengths of tainting your meat just to get you closed down? I know who the most likely culprit was, and I think you do too. The guy who was a known pest. Who was so desperate to open his balloon store he was always haranguing the locals for their lease. Who hounded your landlord so much he ended up saying he could have the lease if you ever left. Preston was the one who tainted the meat and drove you out of business, wasn't he?"

Pete stared at her. His pretend aghast face was so atrocious it belonged on a telenovela.

Ali took her moment. She slammed her coffee cup onto the coaster, making it slosh over the edges, and exclaimed, "Admit it! Admit you wanted revenge!"

Pete broke. All at once, big fat tears starting rolling down his cheeks. Tinkerbell feverishly began licking them as Pete's shoulders shook with emotion.

Ali was stunned. Psychopaths didn't cry. They didn't feel complex emotions like self-pity. They felt rage, not sorrow. Maybe her hunch was wrong. Had she misjudged this whole thing?

Self-doubt swirled inside of her.

But then Pete looked at her with his bloodshot eyes and spluttered, "You're right. You're right. It was me."

CHAPTER TWENTY SEVEN

Ali stared at Pete in disbelief. The room began spinning around her. Had she really just heard what she thought she had? Had Pete really just admitted to killing Preston?

"What happened?" she heard her voice say, though it seemed to be coming from a million miles away, from someone else who was not her.

"Preston had it in for me from day one," Pete whimpered, sniffling on his sobs. "That whole obsession he had with being undercut for the lease? It started with me. I was the one who undercut him. He might've hassled every new store on the boardwalk, but I was the one who bore the worst of it. Because I was the real villain."

He clutched his Chihuahua in his arms like she was a security blanket. Tinkerbell appeared to be finding this whole thing very distressing, flinching every time one of Pete's tears plopped onto her head.

Pete sniffed loudly. "It's very difficult to be the object of someone's hatred for so many years. And it wasn't just me, it was Kerrigan, too. Preston hassled the both of us, everywhere we went."

Ali thought it was pretty rich that he was trying to paint himself as the victim here. She suspected he'd justified the whole thing in his head. That Preston's decades-long campaign of harassment had pushed him right to the brink, and had boiled over one day with unexpected, murderous consequences. And while the years of Preston's torment sounded like a nightmare, that didn't justify his murder. There were far more legal, non-murdery options they could've exhausted first.

"Why didn't you take out a restraining order against him?" Ali asked.

"Kerrigan and I talked about it," Pete sniveled. "But we decided it would be unfair. His mother had Alzheimer's. She relied on him for care. If we'd had him banned from the boardwalk, he wouldn't have been able to get his groceries. I'm not sure if anyone told you, but the man was missing a few screws. He couldn't drive, and he stuck to the same small area, never venturing outside of it. A restraining order would've ruined his life."

Ali was tempted to ask him how resorting to killing the man was in any way better than forcing him to take a different route to a new grocery store, but since Pete was now on a roll, she sat back and let him talk himself into his own hole.

"We tried to endure it," he continued, "Kerrigan and I. But it put us both under enormous stress. Then one day, it all just stopped. I'd not said anything to Preston, so I asked Kerrigan if he had. Kerrigan told me about the promise he'd made to Preston, that if I ever left my store, he'd be next in line for the lease. He knew right away he'd made a terrible mistake. We were both afraid of the implications, of what Preston might do next. I think we instinctively knew he'd do something. And alas, he did."

"He tainted your meat," Ali offered coolly.

Pete nodded pitifully, and started to sob again in earnest.

Ali found it impossible to find any sympathy for him. He could pretend to be a good guy pushed to the brink all he wanted, but she wasn't buying it for a second. None of this was a justification for what he'd done to Preston.

Pete wiped the tears from his eyes with his palms. "A bunch of people got food poisoning. It was a miracle no one died. Once the health inspectors traced the meat back to my pita store, that was it. They didn't care whether I was sabotaged or not, the buck still stopped with me. So they shut me down. I lost my store. My pride and joy. I'd devoted years of my life to making that place a success! And…" His voice lowered with shame. "I guess the only way I can explain what happened next is that I saw red."

Ali shook her head, reviled by what she was hearing.

"You killed him," she said.

Suddenly, Pete's gaze snapped up to meet hers. He looked horrified. Genuinely, this time, not like his awful attempts at acting before.

"What?" he cried. "That's not what I meant! I saw red when you arrived. When your store popped up in place of mine. I—I told everyone your place also had health code violations."

"You did *what*?" Ali cried.

Was that why no one had set foot inside her store?

Pete's eyes darted down with shame. He spoke more quietly. "And I—I encouraged Tinkerbell to do her business outside your store."

Now Ali was completely lost for words. She thought of the neatly coiled dog poop she'd cleaned off her step just this morning. That had been deliberate?

"I thought that was why you came to my house today. To get me to confess. But you were here because you thought—you thought *I* killed Preston?"

He sounded incredulous. Insulted.

Ali's head began spinning with self-doubt.

Had this all been a huge misunderstanding? Had Pete been acting guilty this whole time only because he'd circulated rumors about her and left dog poop outside her store, or was he just using that as an excuse now and playing her for a fool? A double bluff, so to speak.

Ali couldn't make sense of it at all. Pete's acting had been woeful before, and now he seemed completely genuine. Was he just better at acting incredulous than he was at acting shocked? If this was all an act, had Pete gotten Tinkerbell to poop there as a decoy? Then why admit to starting the rumor?

"Why are you just sitting there?" Pete yelled. "I demand an apology!"

"You expect me to apologize to you?" Ali shot back, almost choking on her shock. Now it was her turn to be incredulous. "You just admitted to trying to ruin my business! And leaving dog poop on my doorstep!"

"And you just accused me of being a murderer!" he bellowed.

Ali leapt up off her stool. "Someone killed Preston Lockley, and it wasn't me!" she yelled.

Pete jumped off his stool too, and towered over her. "Well, it wasn't me, either!" he yelled back.

They both stood there, fuming, glaring at one another. Pete's confessions had riled Ali so much, she didn't even feel intimidated by his hulking size. She was filled to the brim with fury and adrenaline.

"Nothing you've told me proves it wasn't you," she said.

Pete's eyes narrowed. "Are you demanding an alibi? Well, I can't give you one because I was at home alone."

She folded her arms. "How convenient."

"Actually, convenient would be that I was out in a public place with lots of witnesses. Instead I was at home watching TV and crying over a dying dragon."

Ali wasn't buying his alibi. There'd been enough spoilers about Raquel the dragon's tragic demise that everyone in the country had heard about it by now, whether they wanted to or not. He'd have to do better than that if he wanted to convince her.

But he didn't get the chance. Their argument was interrupted by a sudden loud, persistent knocking on the front door.

Ali and Pete exchanged a glance, then turned their heads in unison toward the source. Tinkerbell let out a terrified squeak and began trembling in Pete's arms.

"I appear to have a visitor," Pete said coolly. "I think you should leave."

"After you," Ali said, gesturing to the corridor.

She didn't trust Pete not to grab a bottle of wine from his special fancy wine fridge and bop her over the head with it.

The pounding on the door continued. Pete rolled his eyes with defeat and went first. Ali followed along the corridor behind him.

When Pete reached the door, he pulled it open, giving Ali a clear view of who it was standing on the doorstep. She froze to the spot with surprise.

It was Detective Elton.

CHAPTER TWENTY EIGHT

The black-clad woman looked just as surprised to see Ali hovering over Pete's shoulder as Ali was to see her standing on his doorstep.

"What are you doing here?" Detective Elton asked, her husky-voiced question directed at Ali rather than Pete, who was presumably the person she'd actually come here to see.

"Nothing," Ali said quickly. "I was just leaving."

She squeezed past Pete's bulking frame and out through the door.

But as she passed Detective Elton, the woman grasped her arm tightly and tugged her closer.

"Get back to your store, Ms. Sweet," she said in a low whisper. "I don't want to see you meddling in this case again…"

Her warning rang in Ali's ears as she quick-stepped along the sidewalk, bowing her head as she passed the black Mercedes parked up by the curb, attempting not to be spotted by Detective Callihan, who was presumably sitting on the other side of the black-tinted window.

But her attempts to pass covertly were to no avail. She heard the door click open behind her, and Detective Callihan's voice call out, "Ali?"

She paused and turned slowly on the spot to see the preppy detective emerging from the driver's side of the Merc. He jogged over to her, smiling genially.

"What are you doing here?" he asked.

Ali was caught too off guard to make up a lie.

"I was talking to Pete," she said, pointing to the open door where Pete and Detective Elton appeared to be engaged in a very animated discussion.

Detective Callihan looked back at her and smiled. "So you figured it out before we did? I'm impressed."

"Figured what out?"

"Pete," Detective Callihan said. "We were reviewing the security footage of you from the pier that night when we spotted him. Completely destroyed his alibi." He chuckled. "He almost had us fooled with all that Raquel the dragon stuff."

144

Ali's heart began to race. The cops had solid evidence of Pete being at the crime scene? A collapsed alibi and proof he was lying about where he'd been that night? So her hunch had been right after all. Pete had killed Preston out of revenge for the tainted meat scandal, and the whole Tinkerbell poop thing was just a decoy in case she came around with her accusations.

"I guess that means I'm off the hook then?" Ali said.

"It sure does," Detective Callihan said, rocking back on his heels with finality.

Just then, she heard a commotion. She looked up to see Detective Elton leading a very upset Pete toward the Merc behind them. The Marilyn Monroe door was now shut. From behind it came the sound of Tinkerbell's shrill, unhappy barks.

"I'm telling you!" Pete cried as Detective Elton marched him, cuffed, toward the vehicle. "I just went to see my old storefront. I forgot to tell you, that's all."

"We can talk about all the other things you forgot down at the station, can't we?" came Detective Elton's smug reply.

Detective Callihan turned back to Ali. "Oops. Duty calls. Hey, are you still doing your cop coffee discount?"

"Uh-huh," Ali said absentmindedly. Her entire focus was on Pete as he was guided into the back seat.

"Cool. I'll pop in some time."

"Okay…"

Ali wasn't listening at all to Detective Callihan. Because something just didn't feel right about Pete's arrest. Something wasn't adding up. And while she was relieved to be off the cop's suspects list, she didn't want it to come at the expense of an innocent man.

The Merc revved to life. Ali watched as it passed her, peering at the back seat window where Pete was sitting in cuffs, in plain view unlike the detectives up front protected by tinted glass.

She watched the car all the way down the hill, until it turned at the main road and disappeared out of sight.

Ali hurried down the hill after it. Her mind was whirring from the events that had just taken place. She no longer knew what to believe.

As she neared the bottom, she spotted Kerrigan standing on the steps that led up to his yellow door. He looked troubled.

"Ali!" he exclaimed when he spotted her. "You won't believe it. Pete's been arrested!"

"I just saw," Ali said. "I was up the hill… on my lunch break."

145

She figured it wasn't sensible to tell him she'd been present when it happened.

"Did you see what happened?" Kerrigan pressed.

He looked flustered, and patted his sweaty brow with his hand.

"No, not really," Ali said. "Sorry. But I'd better go. I don't want to leave the lunch crowd waiting."

The non-existent lunch crowd, she thought.

She hurried on, leaving Kerrigan behind her as she continued on down the hill.

When she made it onto the boardwalk, she headed in the direction of her bakery, desperate for the quiet sanctuary it would provide her to get her thoughts aligned.

As she drew closer, she saw the tables outside Marco's and Emilio's pizzerias were full to capacity. It only made the big gap in the middle where her store stood look even more pronounced.

Curiously, Ali noticed all the customers were looking in the same direction, and they were chatting animatedly to one another as if something intriguing had just taken place.

"Ali," Marco exclaimed as she approached. "We just saw the strangest thing."

"Pete was in the back of a police car," Emilio interjected.

"He must've been arrested," Marco continued.

"Because of Preston's murder," Emilio said, loudly, trying to drown out his twin even though they were essentially saying the same thing.

Ali squirmed. She couldn't help but feel incredibly responsible for Pete's arrest, as if she'd somehow steered the police in that direction. In a way, she had. They'd been reviewing her security footage after all when they spotted him. If they hadn't been pursuing her in the first place, they might never have spotted him.

It didn't help Ali's paranoia that behind the twins, all their customers were gossiping away and whispering their rumors from table to table.

How long before everyone found out she'd been present during Pete's arrest? How long before they put two and two together and came up with five, shoe-horning in a way to blame her for getting their beloved Pete arrested?

"It could've been over anything," Ali offered, meekly.

"Like what?" Emilio asked, frowning.

"I don't know, maybe there's been a break in the case about his health code violation and they're taking him to the station to chat about it."

"The health code violation!" Marco echoed with aplomb. "That must've been his first attempt at murder!"

"Yes!" Emilio exclaimed, agreeing with his brother for once. His eyes were wide with intrigue. "You think you know someone..."

Well, that backfired, Ali thought.

"I'd better open up," Ali said, rummaging in her pocket for her keys. "I'll see you guys later."

She unlocked the bakery and rushed inside, letting the silence of her store envelop her.

Her mind was a blur. Too much had happened too suddenly for her to wrap her head around it all. She'd gone back and forth in her head about Pete's involvement in Preston's murder more times than a tennis ball in a rally. She needed to untangle this mess in her mind.

She fired up the coffee machine and made a strong espresso, knocking it back like a shot. There was nothing like a dose of caffeine to get the creative juices flowing.

She recalled Delaney's non-dominant hand calming technique, and grabbed the broom in her left hand. She began sweeping the peppermint-green floor tiles, giving her thoughts the space they needed to align.

Which was of course the exact moment her cell phone started to ring. She checked the display screen. It was her mom.

Georgia Sweet had a knack for calling at the worst possible time. It was almost as if she had a telepathic ability to sense her children were in distress, and instinctively intervened, even though her telephone calls tended to be more stress-inducing than supportive.

Ali took a seat at the window and answered the call.

"Ali, darling," her mother began. "I think we need to talk."

CHAPTER TWENTY NINE

Ali's grip on the phone tightened. She felt every fiber in her body tense. As far as openers went, "I think we need to talk" was about as bad as they came. She braced herself for some terrible, disastrous news.

"What do we need to talk about?" Ali asked, meekly.

"It's about this store of yours," came her mom's voice in her ear.

"Uh-huh…"

"And when you're planning on closing it."

Realizing this was one of her mom's life-intervention calls, Ali let out a long, sad sigh. On the good side, she wasn't about to be delivered terrible news. But on the flip side, she was about to get a lecture about her bad life choices.

"Can we not have this talk right now?" she pleaded. "I have a lot on my mind."

"I'm sure you do," Georgia replied. "Teddy filled me in. Darling, I'm very disappointed you accepted all his hard-earned toothpaste commercial money from him. It was lovely for him to offer, but surely you knew there were far wiser ventures for him to invest in than your bakery? You haven't made a buck to show for it."

Ali twisted her lips. She could forgive Teddy for misrepresenting their arrangement. If their mom thought the money he'd given her was an "investment" but was still disappointed she'd accepted it, imagine how much worse she'd be if she realized Teddy had given her it as a gift.

"You do know it's early days," Ali said. "Some businesses don't turn a profit for months."

"I know that. Because like I told you before, Hannah explained to me at length about just how unlikely a bakery on the California coast was to thrive. So this can't be a surprise to you."

Ali rolled her eyes to the ceiling. For a brief second, she expected to see all the same grease splotches she'd come to know from working at Éclairs, and it took a moment to remember that that was all in her past. Because she'd changed her life. She'd taken her dream and run with it.

Couldn't her mom see just how much guts that had really taken? Didn't she want her to be happy?

"I'm following my dream, Mom," Ali said.

"And that's very admirable," Georgia replied. "But all dreams need a cut-off point, don't they? The point where you accept that reality isn't what you thought it would be."

She could say that again. Ali's dream to open a bakery had turned into a nightmare murder investigation. Speaking of, her mom hadn't actually mentioned the dead body. Maybe Teddy had managed not to blab about it. Small mercies.

"I don't think a week should be my cut-off point," Ali said, sounding quite level-headed. "Imagine if Harrison Ford had quit acting when he didn't get his first part. We'd have no Hans Solo."

"Allison!" her mom snapped. "You need to start taking this seriously. You are a grown woman throwing what little money you have at a silly dream."

Ali was taken aback. Trashing her dream was one thing. But calling it silly? That stung.

"I promise you I am taking this deadly seriously," Ali told her. "I studied my ass off to get here."

"Language. And if I recall, you studied to become a pâtissier, not a bakery store owner. Writing a cookbook was on the wish list, if I remember correctly, and creating a line of novelty shaped cupcake casings. But a bakery? That came out of nowhere."

Ali's pulse was starting to race. She knew her mom meant well and that she just wanted the best for her daughter, but Ali really wished she could express it in a kinder manner. It was no surprise that Hannah burnt out as frequently as she did if these were the kind of pep talks she got from their mom every time something went awry.

Ali took a deep breath, trying to keep her emotions at bay. "Mom, I didn't tell you about my bakery dream because I knew you wouldn't approve. You have high aspirations for me, and I do as well. But mine look different from yours. I don't think working for a fancy restaurant in Silverlake is better than being my own boss. It might sound better when you tell your friends over brunch, but this takes a lot of work, too."

"Now you're just making things up," Georgia Sweet replied, sounding displeased. "You can't reinvent the past, darling. I raised you. I was there. I've known all your hopes, fears, and dreams since you were in diapers. It went astronaut, zoologist, chef, in that order. Running a bakery has never been one of them."

"Yes, it has," Ali replied, more firmly. Her gaze traveled out the window and to the bright yellow Ferris wheel at the end of the pier. With a sad, wistful exhale, she added, "But I kept it between me and Dad."

On the other end of the line, silence fell.

"Excuse me?" Georgia said at last.

Ali felt overwhelmed with emotion for her missing father. He didn't speak to her the way her mom did. He was always encouraging and kind. He'd made everything fun. That was the reason she'd only told him, because she knew he wouldn't trash her idea in the same way her mom was about to.

"Dad was the only person I told about my bakery idea," Ali said again.

Her mom let out a scoffing noise of bluster. "I'm surprised you even got the chance, since he was always flitting in and out of your life. And more out than in, let's be honest."

Ali cringed. She really didn't want this to descend into a critique of her father.

"It was when I was in high school," she explained. "Dad asked me about my college plans and I told him about going to culinary school and working in Silverlake and he ... well, he asked me whether they were my plans or yours."

There was a protracted pause. Ali held her breath. She knew her mom wouldn't take her admission well, and she braced herself for the fallout.

When Georgia Sweet spoke again her tone was cold and clipped. "And how did you answer his question?"

Ali's heart raced. Her mom had put her in an uncomfortable position. An impossible one. It wasn't her intention to make her mom feel bad or left out, but she'd been backed into a corner and the only other option, to lie, was no option at all.

"I said they were yours," she replied, her voice small. "And Mom, please know I'm not saying any of this to hurt you. I just need you to understand I didn't make this whole thing up on the spot. It's always been there, lingering at the back of my mind. Even in the astronaut days. Don't you remember getting me those rocket-shaped cookie cutters for Christmas?" She smiled at the memory, and hoped an injection of nostalgia would turn the conversation around.

"No, I don't," Georgia snapped. "I remember rocket-ship pajamas and astronaut Halloween costumes. Honestly, I think you're just making this all up because you don't want to admit I'm right."

Ali's shoulders slumped. She watched the Ferris wheel turning at the end of the pier, its lights flashing brightly.

"You know, Dad was very encouraging about it," she said, mournfully.

"Of course he was," her mom snapped in reply. "Your dad wasn't practical. He was a daydreamer. He had the luxury of encouraging you kids to live in la-la land because he was never there to handle the messy bits of reality." She sounded indignant. "Teddy's obviously a lost cause, pursuing the acting route, but I thought I'd managed to steer you and Hannah in better directions. I thought I'd taught you about the practicalities of life and work and what it actually means to be a responsible adult. But clearly only Hannah was listening. I didn't teach you well enough."

Ali was half tempted to say that if Hannah was the success story among Georgia Sweet's three children, perhaps her values were a little askew. But she didn't get a chance, because her mom was on a tirade and there was no interrupting her.

"Do you know how much debt your father left me with?" she ranted. "How devastating it was for me to be left in the lurch by him, with three children and all his unpaid bills? It's only now he's been declared legally dead that I'm clear of it."

Her words hit Ali like a tsunami. She felt like she was in one of the free-falling rides on the pier, plunging dozens of feet toward the ground. Even the window seat beneath her felt suddenly unstable. It was as if the world had been flipped upside down, and she had nothing to cling on to.

"Dad's dead?" she asked, her voice as small as a child's.

There was hesitation on the line. "Legally. Yes."

"What's the difference?" Ali pressed. "When you boil it down, legally dead means … dead. Gone. Never coming back."

Georgia spoke more gently. "It's been over a decade without any sign of life. No sightings. No bank activity. In missing people cases like your father's, the lack of evidence is evidence in itself. He's gone."

Her use of legalese only made Ali feel worse. This was her *dad* she was talking about, not a missing person case!

"Why didn't you tell me?" Ali asked, feeling wounded. "I would've liked to have known you were having him legally terminated."

151

"Because it doesn't change anything, darling," Georgia replied, firmly. "Your dad isn't any more missing now than he was yesterday or the day before or all the days and months and years before that."

The Ferris wheel became blurry as tears welled in Ali's eyes.

"But he is," she countered. "He is more missing, because now no one's looking for him."

She heard her mom's long sigh through the earpiece. "I'm sorry, darling, but they haven't been for a long time."

Tears began to plop from Ali's eyes, streaking down her cheeks and dripping from her chin. She knew her dad's disappearance hadn't been deemed particularly suspicious by the cops—he had a habit of going off the grid, and a long history of falling in and out of touch with his loved ones—but the fact he was still an open case in some LA cop's in-tray gave Ali that sliver of hope that he may one day be traced. But now she could picture his file with a big, red *DECEASED* stamped across the front in block letters, and locked away in a filing cabinet never to be seen again.

"That's not the point," Ali squeaked.

"I'm sorry," Georgia said softly.

"For not telling me?" Ali demanded. "Or for declaring him dead in the first place?"

"I'm sorry for the way you found out," Georgia Sweet said. "But I don't regret doing it, darling. It was the right thing to do."

Ali removed the phone from her ear and pressed her thumb onto the disconnect button. She and her mom clearly had very different definitions of the word *right*.

She stared down at the black screen of her cell phone. The call with her mom had left a very bitter taste in her mouth. Betrayed was perhaps too strong a word for it, but she was definitely hurt by her mom's actions. Her dad had ceased being a husband to Georgia Sweet long before he'd given up on being a parent to his children, but she should have realized just how insensitive declaring him dead behind their backs really was.

She wanted to call Teddy and speak to him about it, but his relationship with their dad had been fraught. And it wasn't worth talking to Hannah, because she always put up one of her big emotion-blocking brick walls when it came to matters involving their father.

Ali would have to look for support closer to home.

Nate had told her she could always talk to him, but since her mood had been up and down like a yo-yo recently, she would prefer not to risk leaving an unstable-woman impression on him. Delaney, of course, would be a wonderful counselor, but it would take more than a cup of chamomile tea and some left-handed coloring to deal with this level of pain.

"I need an emotional support animal," Ali muttered to herself.

That's when she was hit by sudden inspiration. Scruff! Where was that pooch when she needed him?

She headed out of the store, flipping the "closed" sign over on her way, even though no one cared where she was, and locked the door behind her.

"Scruff," she called softly, peeping around the trash cans on the sidewalk for the friendly fur ball. "Where've you got to, scamp?"

The dog was always hanging around in the streets waiting for food, yet when she needed him, he was nowhere to be found.

She wandered under the hot California sun, calling Scruff's name softly as she went. She should've brought a pastry with her. She bet he'd come running the second he smelled food.

Speaking of smelling food, a gorgeous aroma was wafting along the boardwalk toward her—freshly baked dough and Italian herbs. She sniffed the air. Her stomach growled as the smell of delicious pizza filled her nostrils and overwhelmed her senses, and she realized she hadn't stopped to eat yet today. She had no choice but to follow her nose.

She drew up outside a pizzeria she'd never been in and was about to march straight in through the glass door and order a fresh margherita, when she paused. Standing in the middle of the joint was a group of shady-looking men. It wasn't just their slicked-back hair, suits, and chunky gold jewelry that made Ali hesitant, but the way they held themselves, the way they were bundled together, like they were conspiring. The decor of the pizzeria didn't help matters, either; it was fifties inspired with big red booths providing a distinctly mob-like setting.

Ali began to slowly back away.

Just then, she heard a bark from behind her. She turned around. Scruff was sitting on the sidewalk, wagging his tail across the slabs, panting happily.

"There you are," Ali said. "I've been looking for you. I need a therapy session. How does one jumbo bone sound in exchange for me off-loading all my woes?"

Scruff barked as if accepting her terms.

Ali was about to head off back down the sidewalk when the sound of a store bell tinkling behind her made her halt.

"You're the baker," a voice said from behind her.

Ali flinched. Slowly, she turned back around.

The glass door of the pizzeria was now open, and standing in the doorway, staring at her with menacing expressions, were three suited men.

Ali gulped.

As her gaze roved from one pair of mean dark eyes to the next, she caught a flash of light above their head and peered up. A flashing sign above the door said: *Fat Tony's*.

CHAPTER THIRTY

Standing before Ali was a short guy, with an oblong face. He slowly looked her up and down.

Is this Fat Tony? Ali thought. *The pizzeria property mogul?*

"You are the woman from the new bakery, aren't you?" he asked.

"Uh-huh," Ali squeaked.

She tried to inch back but there was a fire hydrant blocking her path.

"We've been looking for you," a second man said. This one was tall and lanky, with jet black hair gelled back.

"You have?" Ali replied, her voice barely there. "Because of my coffee discount for local business owners?"

The men exchanged smirks.

"No, actually," the oblong-faced man said. "We wanted to thank you."

"Thank me?" Ali repeated. That wasn't what she'd been expecting. "What for?"

"For solving Preston's murder. It was thanks to you that Pete got arrested, wasn't it?"

"I—I guess."

"Well, Fat Tony's thrilled," the man with jet black hair said. "The cops were going to pin it on him, since he'd just opened up a new place for Giuseppe, and Preston was in there harassing him. But thanks to you, the real perp's been caught." He clapped his hands together as if wiping dirt from them. "Poof. The problem disappeared."

Ali was stunned. It felt like a shockwave through her. Fat Tony had recently opened a new pizzeria? And Preston had been in there hassling the owner?

The way he emphasized *real* seemed to suggest to her that they knew exactly who the real perp was, and that it wasn't Pete at all.

"Tony—Tony opened a new store?" she asked.

"That's right, lady. What's wrong? It looks like you've seen a ghost."

"Can you tell me where it is?" Ali said, maneuvering clumsily around the fire hydrant as she backed away from the store.

"Other end of the boardwalk."

"Thanks, It's been a pleasure," she said, spinning on her heel and hurrying away.

Scruff followed alongside her and the sound of the men's cackles seemed to follow her the whole way along the sidewalk in pursuit of Fat Tony's new pizzeria.

*

Ali's heart was pounding as she hurried along the boardwalk. That was the second time she'd heard Fat Tony's name in relation to Preston, and what the mobster-looking men had told her back at the pizzeria was making her extremely suspicious.

This was so much bigger than she'd anticipated. Getting mixed up with the mob was a very bad idea. But what choice did she have?

She marched along the boardwalk as fast as she could. Fast enough to give Irene and the neon power walkers a run for their money. The heat bore down on her, but Ali was determined to find this new pizzeria.

Nate had missed the place out of his list of new establishments that had recently opened, so she'd never been inside to speak to the owner or test their alibi. If Preston launched a scathing attack on this Giuseppe guy like the one he'd launched on Ali, perhaps he'd messed with the wrong guy. Of course Fat Tony would be thrilled that she'd gotten a man jailed for it, because it let them off the hook.

Scruff panted as he ran alongside her. He seemed to be enjoying all this excitement, and was completely oblivious to the terrible danger Ali had now suddenly found herself in.

Oh, to be a dog, she thought, desperately.

Suddenly, she saw it. Giuseppe's. Beneath the sign was the tagline: *Fat Tony's Thin Cousin.*

It had the exact same decorative style as the pizzeria Ali had just left. The boardwalk was literally flanked either side by Fat Tony.

She noticed inside, this joint had another bunch of shady-looking mob guys. It was like Groundhog Day. These guys looked far more menacing than the other ones.

Sitting at the table was an enormous man, and through the window, Ali caught sight of a letter tattooed across each of his fingers. T-O-N-Y.

It was him. It was Fat Tony himself.

Ali gasped and moved back from the window, discreetly watching the people inside. Fat Tony appeared to be talking on a cell phone.

Then suddenly, he turned his head to the window and his eyes locked on her.

Ali's heart went into her throat. She wanted to run, but fear had frozen her to the spot. She stood there helpless as Fat Tony stood from the table, waddled to the door, and pulled it open.

"My boys just called," he said, stepping out. "They told me to expect a visit from you."

Ali trembled as Fat Tony walked toward her, his hands outstretched.

All she could do was close her eyes. She squeezed them tight, not wanting to look into the eyes of her murderer as he suffocated her life out of her.

She felt Fat Tony's warm hands on her cheeks and flinched with terror. But rather than snapping her neck in his meaty hands, he kissed both her cheeks.

"Come in!" he exclaimed jovially, in the thickest Italian-American accent Ali had ever heard. "You get free pizza for life!"

He released her from his grasp.

Ali staggered back, astonished, and blinked at the enormous gangster in front of her.

"I'm sorry, wh—what?" she stammered.

Fat Tony's grin stretched from ear to ear. "You got the police off my back, right? So come in. Let's eat. Celebrate."

He slung an arm around her and cajoled her toward the store. Ali's feet seemed to stagger beneath her. She had no choice but to be led inside.

Ali wasn't sure if this was the bravest thing she'd ever done in her life, or the stupidest, but she followed Fat Tony inside.

CHAPTER THIRTY ONE

Giuseppe, Fat Tony's thin cousin, dumped a margherita pizza on the table in front of Ali. It wafted its steamy scents of basil into her nostrils. She stared down at it, too scared to even take a bite despite how hungry she was and how delicious it looked. Fat Tony and his gang may well be behaving toward her with hospitality, but that didn't mean they hadn't poisoned the pizza or something.

"Aren't you going to eat?" Fat Tony asked, sinking his large body into the seat opposite her.

Ali swallowed hard, feeling pinned by his gaze. She felt like she was in the weirdest job interview. One where you weren't just discussing your salary expectations, but whether you'd be allowed to walk out the door alive…

"I—already had lunch," she lied. "Maybe you could put it in a doggy bag for me, and I'll have it later?"

Fat Tony blinked at her. Then his face cracked with amusement and he let out a huge belly laugh.

"Did you hear that, boys? She wants a doggy bag!"

The wall of mobsters standing shoulder to shoulder behind him chuckled on cue. But not a single one of them smiled.

Ali's nerves spiked.

"Mind if I eat while we talk?" Fat Tony said.

"Be my guest," Ali replied.

She watched as Fat Tony took a huge slice of glistening pizza and began to munch. It really did look like exceptionally good pizza. If the restaurant was a front for some shady criminal operation, they'd done an excellent job of covering it up.

"What do you think of my new pizzeria?" Fat Tony asked her, his mouth full. He gestured with his arms.

"It's great," Ali replied immediately, without even glancing around. She knew what Fat Tony wanted to hear, and since she wanted to walk out of here alive, she readily obliged.

"We opened the same day as your bakery," Fat Tony continued. "You see, my cousin needed some help getting back on his feet after a... little mishap. Family is family. So I leased him this place."

Ali's gaze briefly flicked to Giuseppe. He was standing blank-faced behind Fat Tony, a telltale twitch beneath his left eye that told Ali he was holding back. She didn't even want to imagine what his so-called "little mishap" had entailed, but guessed it wasn't anything legal.

"That's nice of you," Ali squeaked, shifting in her chair.

"I'm a nice guy," Fat Tony replied, flashing her a smile that looked far more sinister than nice. Grease shimmered on his lips.

Ali looked down at the blobs of margherita on her pizza, trying to focus on anything but that mean face scrutinizing her.

"It's a lovely bit of coast to own property on," he continued, racing through yet another slice of pizza. "I've got about a dozen buildings in my portfolio now. One day, I'll own the whole boardwalk. Then the pier. Then the town."

Ali silently prayed that day would never actually come. The thought of Fat Tony being her landlord instead of blustering Kerrigan O'Neal filled her with dread.

A void of silence surrounded them, filled only with the sound of Fat Tony chewing on his pizza crusts. The whole while he ate, he stared at Ali emotionlessly. Ali felt like he might swallow her up at any moment.

"So?" Fat Tony said at last, grabbing his last slice of pizza and using it to gesture at Ali. "When are you going to ask the question?"

Grease splattered onto the tabletop. Ali flinched. Her heart began pounding.

"The question?" she asked, nervously.

Fat Tony rolled his eyes nonchalantly and waved his pizza slice around. "The question. The question. About Preston. The guy found floating with the fishes. We all know that's why you came here. Why you were poking your nose around."

Ali gulped. Fat Tony was goading her to ask him if he'd knocked off Preston. Practically daring her.

Ali's instincts to get up and run away had never been so strong. But she fought them off. She was about to finally get her answer. If the mob were going to kill her, she'd prefer to go out knowing the truth.

"Okay," Ali said, swallowing nothing, since her mouth was completely dry. "Did you?"

A slow smile inched its way across Fat Tony's lips. He lowered his face.

"Did I what?" he pressed.

"Kill him," Ali clarified. "Did you kill Preston Lockley?"

Fat Tony leaned back in his chair, making it squeak in protest under his huge frame. Slowly, he wiped the grease off his fingers with a napkin, one at a time. He was biding his time. Making her sweat. And boy was she sweating! Ali had never felt fear quite like this in her life. It seemed her body's only way of responding to the spike in adrenaline and cortisol was to open up every pore in her skin and let the sweat come flooding out of it.

Finally, apparently satisfied that his fingers were clean, Fat Tony put his crumpled napkin on his plate and began to speak.

"I had the opportunity," he said, nodding his head. "And the means." He pointed at the men behind him and grinned. Then he opened his hands out wide. "But what was my motive? Why would I want to kill Preston Lockley?"

He spoke with the cadence of a teacher, and it took Ali a moment to realize his question wasn't rhetorical. He actually wanted her to guess what his motive for murder might be.

"Because he annoyed you?" she suggested.

Tony steepled his hands over his pizza. "Do I look like the sort of guy who can't handle a mild annoyance?" He shook his head. "Try again, Blondie."

Ali wracked her brains. If this was Fat Tony's way of telling her he wasn't the culprit, it was painfully convoluted. And if this whole thing ended in her being executed anyway, what was the point of this charade? He was clearly getting his kicks out of watching her squirm.

"Because he threatened your store?" she tried.

Now Tony laughed. "Balloon man? A threat? Hardly." Behind him, his cronies laughed too. "Any other guesses?"

Ali had to admit it. Tony was obviously a shady guy with some dodgy dealings going on, but he had no reason to kill Preston. Unless...

"He insulted you," she suggested, the idea coming to her all at once.

Fat Tony stayed as solid as before. But Ali noticed something else. Giuseppe was starting to look flustered. The twitch under his eye was going at a thousand miles a second.

Ali mind raced as she assessed Giuseppe's sudden shift in demeanor. The cousin who'd been leased the pizzeria in spite of his prior unspecified "little mishap" was suddenly agitated, shifting from foot to foot like he wanted to be anywhere else but here.

160

Ali realized she was onto something. Fat Tony might not feel threatened or easily offended by a man like Preston Lockley coming around making a ruckus, but what about Giuseppe? It was the thin cousin who'd been on the receiving end of Preston's tirade, after all, not Fat Tony. Giuseppe had been the one standing behind the counter being accosted by an angry stranger about a lease, getting the "Preston Lockley treatment," as Nate called it. Ali knew herself from personal experience just how unpleasant that was. Maybe Giuseppe wasn't as level-headed as his obese cousin.

Filled with confidence, Ali kept her gaze on Fat Tony as she spoke, but secretly directed her words to Giuseppe, who was squirming behind him.

"Did Preston disrespect you?" Ali asked. "Insult your family? Your pizza? Do you have a temper? A history of violence? A record of not being able to control yourself? Some past... *little mishaps*?"

Suddenly, Fat Tony's brow furrowed. At the mention of the key words "little mishaps," a look of realization overcame him.

He swiveled in his chair, the wood straining beneath his sudden movement, and focused on the fidgeting man behind him.

Giuseppe went bright red. The telltale sign of guilt.

"Giuseppe!" Fat Tony yelled, heaving his enormous body to standing so suddenly his chair fell back and hit the floor with a dramatic crash. "Did *you* kill the balloon man?"

Giuseppe put his hands in the air. "I didn't mean to, Tony, I really didn't."

He had the same thick accent as his cousin, but his voice was weaselly, high-pitched and nasally.

Ali watched, astonished, as the truth came tumbling from his thin lips.

"He came in here yelling at me," Giuseppe said, "just like you said he would. And I let him go, just like you told me to."

"Then what happened?" Fat Tony said through his clenched teeth. "To make you go against my clear and expressed conditions?"

"Well, I bumped into him on the pier," Giuseppe continued. "And he started up again. And this time he really pressed my button, Tony." He clenched his fists and shook his head, as if riled up all over again by the memory replaying in his head. "He insulted the pizza. He insulted Nonna's recipe."

Fat Tony made a cross on his chest at the mention of their presumably deceased grandmother. Then he switched straight back into frustrated, disappointed mob boss mode.

He rubbed his forehead like this was all giving him a headache. Like Giuseppe had caused a massive inconvenience and he needed to find a way to fix it.

Ali, on the other hand, was utterly flabbergasted by the turn of events. Preston Lockley had been murdered by a mobster because he'd insulted his grandma's pizza recipe?

"How are we supposed to clean up this mess?" Fat Tony muttered aloud, shaking his head.

"We don't," Giuseppe said. "Because someone's already in jail for it."

Ali was about to protest against them leaving Pete in jail to take the rap for it, then remembered who she was dealing with and kept mum.

"This time, sure," Fat Tony said. "But what about next time someone insults Nonna's pizza recipe? What then? I gave you a chance because you promised me you wouldn't kill anyone again. And it took you a day to break that promise."

Again? Ali thought with a grimace. Was that Giuseppe's prior "little mishap"? Murder?

Fat Tony continued. "We can't have you bumping off every unhappy customer. It's bad for business. You're a loose cannon, Giuseppe. We can't have loose cannons in our gang."

Ali's eyes widened as she realized what Fat Tony was implying. She leapt to her feet, ready to make a run for it if bullets started raining down.

It took Giuseppe a little longer to cotton on, but when the horrified dawning overcame his features, his skin turned pallid as the blood drained from it.

Suddenly, moving like a bolt of lightning, Giuseppe ran for the door.

He shoved past Ali in his haste to get out, and she staggered back, almost tripping. One of Fat Tony's mobsters caught her by the elbow, righting her and smiling politely, before streaking out the store in pursuit of the fleeing Giuseppe.

The pizzeria cleared out in a matter of seconds, leaving just Fat Tony and Ali inside. Ali motioned for the door, but the fat mobster held his hand up to stop her.

"You don't want to see," he said, in a grandfatherly kind of tone.

162

Ali halted. This entire thing was messing with her head.

She waited for some kind of sound that would tell her Giuseppe had met a grisly end, but instead of beatings or gunfire, she heard the loud barking of a dog.

Fat Tony looked at her, confused. He dropped the hand he'd been using to halt her. Ali could tell by his face that things weren't going the way he'd anticipated.

"What now…" he muttered, shaking his head.

Together, they paced over to the door and peered out.

Giuseppe was lying on the sidewalk very much alive, writhing and crying out. To Ali's surprise, the reason for his distress was not a beating from his former gang members, but Scruff the dog. The furry little scamp had his jaws clamped around Giuseppe's ankle, making the man writhe in agony. All the mobsters who'd been chasing him before were standing around guffawing their heads off.

"Oi!" Fat Tony bellowed across the street at them. "What are you doing?"

His gang jumped like a bunch of unruly kids getting shouted at in the schoolyard. They looked at Tony uncertainly.

Fat Tony threw his arms in the air with annoyance. "Kill him!"

"But boss," one of the men said, pointing at Scruff and his sharp teeth latched around Giuseppe's ankle. "There's a dog."

"I don't care!" Fat Tony screamed. "Kill the dog if you have to!"

"No!" Ali cried. "Please don't hurt the dog. He's a … friend of mine."

Tony looked at her with a peculiar expression, then huffed. "Fine. Don't kill the dog!"

His gang looked relieved. But they were still hesitant to approach Scruff. They danced around awkwardly, trying to find a way in to begin their attack, then jumping back when they got too close to Scruff's jaws.

Suddenly flashing lights appeared at the end of the street. Someone must've heard all the commotion and called the cops.

The gangsters looked hapless as they exchanged glances. Then they abandoned the scene, fleeing in all different directions.

"Imbeciles," Fat Tony yelled, thumping his fist on the door frame. "There's a reason why they say if you want something done, do it yourself," he lamented.

He reached for his pocket, and Ali caught a glimpse of a leather gun holster at his hip.

"Wait!" Ali cried, stopping him before he did anything hasty. "You can't shoot him. The cops are right there."

Fat Tony regarded her with skepticism and curiosity, as if trying to work out if this was a trick or not. Then he nodded slowly, and withdrew his hand from the gun he'd been reaching for.

"You don't need Giuseppe dead to get him out of the picture," Ali continued. "You just need him in prison, right?"

"Yes," Fat Tony said. Then he sucked air between his teeth. "I don't know if you know, but there's a reason why you never see guys who look like me standing in witness boxes at court. Families like mine avoid cops and courts and judges and all that stuff at all costs. None of us are going to be witnesses to his confession."

"I could be the witness," Ali said. "I was there when he confessed, too, and I don't mind talking to courts or cops or judges."

She glanced up the road where the black Mercedes was pulling to the curb beside where Scruff and Giuseppe were grappling.

"Besides," she added, looking back at the round-cheeked mobster, "I know those guys."

Fat Tony looked unconvinced. But all Ali cared about was stopping Giuseppe from becoming another senseless murder victim in Willow Bay. One was more than enough to last her for a lifetime.

"Well?" Ali pressed. "Want to leave this one to me?"

Finally, Fat Tony nodded.

"It's all yours, Blondie," he said, retreating back to his pizzeria, tapping his nose as he disappeared.

His was one secret Ali intended to keep.

She turned back to the scene. Detective Elton was talking into her walkie-talkie—calling animal control and an ambulance—while Detective Callihan cautiously attempted to manage the situation. Ali had no idea how she'd managed to get herself caught up in the mob's affairs, but if it was the only way to stop the killing, then she was prepared to do what she must.

She took a deep breath and steeled herself, then exited Fat Tony's pizzeria and trotted toward the two detectives.

"Hey! Guys!" she cried, waving her hand over her head. "This is the man who killed Preston Lockley!"

CHAPTER THIRTY TWO

Hours later, after giving the police her report and going back to her store, Ali stood in her empty bakery. She might be able to solve a murder case, but she still couldn't make a sale if her life depended on it. And thanks to Pete spreading malicious rumors around about the state of hygiene in her store, she might never get a chance. Her Willow Bay adventure may be over before it had really ever began.

Just then, the door flew open, making the bell jangle angrily, and in rushed Teddy.

"Teddy?" Ali said from behind the counter, taken aback at the unexpected appearance of her brother. "What are you doing here?"

She'd texted him as soon as the situation with Giuseppe and the police was over, but hadn't expected him to immediately drop everything and drive all the way here from Venice Beach.

Teddy ran right up to her and swept her into a bone-crushing hug. "Ali-cat! What's wrong? Are you okay? Are you having a medical emergency?"

He released her and took her by the shoulders, staring into each of her eyes as if looking for signs of sickness.

"I'm fine," Ali said, perplexed by his questions. "Just a little shaken up after what happened."

"Tell me what happened," he asked, sounding utterly flummoxed.

"There's not really anything to tell. I said it all in my text."

Teddy raised a single eyebrow and produced his cell phone.

"This text?" he said, flashing the screen her way. *"Solved the case scruff bitman, was mop!,"* he read aloud. "I'm sure you can forgive me for panicking when that garbled message arrived in my inbox."

"Oh," Ali said, embarrassed.

She'd been so shaken up she'd had no idea what she'd typed. Clearly, a load of gobbledygook without punctuation.

"What I was trying to say was that I solved the case," she explained. "Scruff—the dog, the stray I told you about—he bit the man. As in the killer."

Teddy narrowed his eyes and nodded along, as if trying to make sense of what she was telling him. "And what about the bit about the mop?"

"Mob," Ali corrected. "I was meant to write mob."

The color drained from Teddy's face. "*Mob?!*" he screeched.

"Shh!" Ali said, using both her hands to hush him. "Don't go shouting it aloud! Someone might hear."

Teddy clapped a hand over his mouth. He glanced over each shoulder, looking absolutely terrified.

Then he moved his fingers apart and whispered through the gap. "Are you kidding me, Ali? The killer was part of the mob? And you got him caught? You're going to get your legs broken. Or your ears cut off." He grabbed her hand and began yanking her toward the door. "We have to go. Leave the business and the apartment. Go into witness protection."

Ali dug her heels in, resisting his attempts to drag her out of the bakery. "Teddy, calm down!"

"Calm down?" Teddy yelled, forgetting all about being quiet. "The mob is after you."

"No, they're not," she told him firmly. She pulled her arm free of his grip. "The guy was new. And he messed up by killing Preston and putting Fat Tony on the police's radar. Fat Tony's actually glad I interfered."

"F—Fat Tony?" Teddy echoed, looking hypnotized. "I think I need to sit down."

He dropped himself into a seat and stared into the middle distance, looking like he was in complete shock.

"I'll get you some water," Ali told her stricken brother.

She hurried to the kitchen.

Poor Teddy, she thought as she filled a glass with water. *It's a lot to take in.*

She returned to the store to give Teddy his water, but just as she entered, the bell over the door tinkled again. This time, a blur of gorgeous, tanned skin and blond hair entered.

"Nate?" Ali said, her mouth instantly going dry at the sight of the handsome surfer. "What are you doing here?"

Nate looked confused, his thick blond brows drawn together into a frown.

"I just saw Pete," he said, jabbing his thumb over his shoulder. "Looks like the police released him."

166

Ali let out a breath of relief. "Oh, thank goodness. That's a relief."

Despite his attempts to sabotage her business, Ali didn't want an innocent man languishing in prison for no reason.

Nate flashed her querying eyes. "I don't get it. I thought he killed Preston. That's what everyone around town was saying."

Ali shook her head. "It wasn't him. It was Giuseppe, from the new pizzeria."

"There's a new pizzeria?" Nate asked.

"Not anymore, I guess," Ali replied with a shrug.

Just then, Nate spotted Teddy sitting like a statue staring at nothing. "Is that guy bothering you?" he whispered under his breath.

Ali chuckled. "Actually, that's my brother. He just got some shocking news is all."

She suddenly remembered the glass of water she'd fetched for him, and placed it on the tabletop before him. Teddy took one look at it, then turned his haunted eyes up to Ali.

"Got anything stronger?" he asked.

"Yeah, you might want to give him some whiskey or something," Nate said, sounding concerned for the strange zombie-like man.

"Good idea," Ali replied. "I could do with one myself after the day I've had." Realizing this may well be the last chance she had to spend time with Nate, she boldly added, "Want to join us?"

Nate smiled. He took an uncertain look at the zombie that was Teddy. "You sure?"

"He'll perk up once he's got a couple of shots in him," Ali replied.

Nate shrugged. "Okay, sure, if that's cool with you."

Ali went to the kitchen to fetch the bottle of rum she used to flambé with, wondering as she went what her future now held. She may well have worked out who killed Preston Lockley and helped the local mobster resolve his problems, but none of that was exactly going to ingratiate her with the locals. And even if she asked Pete to vouch for her and explain he'd made up those rumors about her health violations, why would anyone listen? He'd presumably lost a lot of respect among the locals after being seen carted off in the back of a cop car.

She walked back into the bakery, gazing wistfully at the bistro tables she'd sourced and the chairs she'd prettily upholstered. She looked forlornly at the display fridge filled with wasted pastries. Her days here were numbered. It was inevitable. It would only be a matter of time before she had to pack up and leave.

She sighed heavily, and went over to the window seat with the bottle. She poured three shot glasses with rum and pushed them across the window table. As she did, she spotted something out the window behind Nate. It was a very forlorn-looking Scruff, standing on the sidewalk watching her through the window with his tail hanging low with dejection.

Ali's heart leapt. It was her furry hero!

She leapt from the table and hurried to the door. "Scruff! Come inside! You were the hero today!"

Scruff let out an excited yip, wagging his tail eagerly as he came bounding inside.

"I don't have any bones for you," she said. "But I do have some berries."

She'd been planning on making mixed berry turnovers, but that wasn't going to happen now. Better not to let them go to waste.

She went again to the kitchen to fetch a ceramic bowl. She filled it with berries and took it to the table, setting it beside Teddy. Scruff looked perplexed for a moment, before he jumped up onto the window seat and happily began chomping away.

Ali took her seat beside him. If it hadn't been for the dire financial situation she was soon to face, and the fact her business dreams were now in tatters, she would've found it rather amusing, the sight of the four of them at the table. They certainly made a peculiar bunch.

Teddy downed his rum and poured another. "So if this Giuseppe fella's in the clink, does that mean you're off the hook?" he asked.

Nate looked surprised at the first words he'd heard come out of the strange zombie-man's lips. "I'm sorry, what?" he asked.

Ali hesitated. She didn't much feel like explaining the whole debacle. And while she was of course relieved to be in the clear, it didn't stop the creeping reality that her time in Willow Bay was almost up.

"There's no point going into it," Ali told Nate. "Preston's killer was caught, so I'm not being investigated by the cops anymore."

Nate looked elated. "But Ali, this is wonderful news! Now you can focus on making this place a success, instead of having to spend all your time clearing your name."

Ali sighed sadly. Her mom's sharp words during their phone call repeated in her mind. Her dream *was* silly, and now Ali had to admit defeat.

"It's too late for that," Ali said. "My rent's due on the apartment and the store soon, and I've barely sold a thing. I can't pay for either."

Saying it aloud made it more real, and Ali felt her shoulders slump sadly with the reality. Scruff nudged her with his nose, as if to cheer her up. But nothing would cheer Ali. She may have won the battle, but she'd lost the war.

Just then, the door flew open, so fast it made everyone jump in their seats.

Scruff barked angrily as the hurricane of Delaney came rushing in. She was panting heavily, like she'd run all the way here from Little Bits of This and That.

"Ali!" she cried, her jewelry jangling as she hurried to the table where the three of them sat. "Did you hear?"

Ali raised her shot glass. "Pete's been released. Giuseppe was the killer. Why don't you sit down and have some rum with us? We're celebrating. Or commiserating, depending on which way you look at it."

Delaney looked perplexed. "What are you talking about?" Then she shook her head. "It doesn't matter. There's no time to explain. Turn on the radio!"

Ali frowned.

Delaney flapped her hands frantically. "Now! Before it's too late!"

Confused, Ali obeyed Delaney's command, going over to the counter and turning the radio on.

After the static cleared, a familiar voice floated out from it. It was an enthusiastic male voice. Ali recognized it from somewhere.

"Is that… Mr. Positive?" she exclaimed, remembering the man who'd so enthusiastically enjoyed her comfort cupcakes.

She couldn't believe it. Mr. Positive was a radio show host?

"Shhhh!" Delaney cried.

Ali pressed her lips together and listened to the voice coming from the radio.

"I'm telling you, folks. These lemon coconut cupcakes were the most divine thing I've tasted in my entire life," he was saying.

Ali couldn't believe it. Was he talking about *her* lemon coconut cupcakes? Her eyes widened as she focused on the voice. Everything else blurred into the background.

"The name of the bakery again is Seaside Sweets," Mr. Positive's voice crackled out. "And it's just opened up on the boardwalk in

Willow Bay. Well worth a trip, and the well-deserving winner of this weekend's Randy Recommends! Now, over to Sheila for the news."

As the female radio host began her news report Ali turned, stunned, to face the others.

Her mouth hung open with surprise. She'd served a cupcake to a local radio host, who'd recommended her to his audience! She could hardly process it.

Teddy and Nate looked fittingly impressed that Ali had earned herself a shout out from the local radio host, but Delaney's expression was so much more than that. She was thrilled, excited, bordering on manic. She grabbed Ali's hand, squeezing it tightly.

"Don't you understand what this means?" she said.

"Ow!" Ali exclaimed, trying to free herself.

But Delaney wasn't letting go. "This is a big deal. Like a crazy big deal. I've been listening to Randy Recommends since I was a kid. He's a Willow Bay institution. People hang off his every word. Whenever he recommends things, they blow up. One year he recommended moccasins and I swear everyone in town bought a pair."

Bemused, Ali's eyes darted over her shoulder to Teddy and Nate. They both looked as equally perplexed as Ali herself was feeling.

Delaney tightened her already bone-crushing grip on Ali's hands, making Ali wince. "Thousands of people tune in to his show every week!" she bellowed, punctuating each word like she was talking to a room full of morons. "Thousands!

Slowly, it began to dawn on Ali what Delaney was telling her. Randy the radio host had a lot of sway in the town. Getting a shout out from him on his show wasn't just a bit of free advertising, it was an endorsement. Pete might not have been able to save her reputation, but Randy could!

Ali fixed her eyes on Delaney. "Did you say th—thousands?"

Delaney's blue eyes sparkled. "Yes! And they'll all be coming by your store tomorrow to try your lemon and coconut cupcakes!"

She looked just about ready to explode. But it was all too much for Ali to take in. Five minutes ago, she was drowning her sorrows in rum she'd never get to flambé and feeding all the berries for the turnovers to a stray dog! Now Delaney was telling her there was still a chance to save the bakery? And that in order to do so, she'd have to pull off some impossible feat of marathon cupcake baking?

"But Delaney," Ali said, shaking her head. "I don't even sell cupcakes."

Delaney grinned from ear to ear. "You do now!"

Her friend grabbed Ali's crumpled apron from the counter and chucked it at her. Despite her spinning mind, Ali managed to catch the little tornado. She stared at it helplessly.

"Chop chop," Delaney declared. "There's no time to waste."

"B—but I don't have a cupcake menu," Ali stammered. "A price plan. I haven't tested flavors. I don't know how to display them."

"None of that matters," Delaney said. "Just do whatever it is you did before to get Randy's endorsement."

Ali grew exasperated. Delaney wasn't getting it. Ali couldn't just whip up a thousand cupcakes overnight. Now she was really starting to panic at the enormity of the task ahead of her. And what would come of it anyway? She wasn't a cupcake store. One crazy day selling cupcakes wasn't going to be enough to save the store if she couldn't follow it up with more.

"I don't sell cupcakes!" Ali cried.

Finally, Delaney stopped. As Ali's yell reverberated around the store, Nate looked awkwardly at the ground. Scruff quirked his head to the side and let out a confused noise.

Teddy, having finally snapped out of his state, hurried over to Ali's side.

"It's okay," he soothed her.

"I just made that batch as comfort food," she told him. "Because it reminded me of Dad."

Teddy let a beat pass. "I know," he said softly. "And do you know what? Dad would be crazy proud if he could be here to see you. This was your dream. The one you told only him about. And you have a chance to make it happen."

His words were comforting, but Ali still resisted.

"Seaside Sweets is meant to be a patisserie," she said in a meek voice. "That's what I trained for. That's what all those years at culinary school were for. I didn't spend a year working with Milo Baptiste to make cupcakes."

She felt a little ashamed to admit it. She knew it made her sound snooty.

Teddy raised an eyebrow. "Are those Mom's words, or yours?"

His statement struck her. Her father had said almost exactly the same thing when challenging her plan to go to culinary school. When she'd been that high schooler, profiteroles and macarons hadn't even been in her vocabulary. When she'd first dreamed up this idea, it had been all about cake.

Just then, Nate approached, looking cautious, like Ali was a bear he didn't want to poke. "If people want cupcakes, Ali, there's nothing wrong with giving them cupcakes."

"He's right," Delaney added. "The people of Willow Bay want comfort food too. You've given people plenty of chances to buy your fancy French pastries if they wanted them."

It was harsh but true. No one wanted her gourmet, high-end, "Victorian French" desserts. They wanted simple, fuss-free cupcakes. As loath as Ali was to admit it, Miriyam had been right all along.

Nate was right, too, about giving the people what they wanted. Teddy was right about Ali's dream being polluted by her mom's opinions. They were all right. All three of them.

As Ali looked from one face to the next, she felt overwhelmed by the support and encouragement they were giving her. If this was her one chance at saving her dream life in Willow Bay, and getting to live out her days with these good people by her side, then she was going to grab hold of it and not let go.

A fire erupted inside of her. She was going to save the store. That would be her new niche. The simple pleasures. It was a good way to approach life, in general.

"Okay," she muttered, giving in. "Okay. I'm doing it. I'm making cupcakes."

Everyone began to cheer and holler. Scruff started running around in circles, barking away happily in response to their sudden ebullience. Every nerve in Ali's body was jangling with a mixture of excitement and apprehension.

There was just one problem. How the heck was she going to pull this off?

Ali stopped jumping. "How am I going to make thousands of cupcakes by tomorrow?"

A grin appeared on Delaney's face. She grabbed three more aprons, chucking one at Nate and another at Teddy, before looping the third one over her head and tying it securely at her waist. "We'll help. So, Chef, what first?"

CHAPTER THIRTY THREE

Ali woke herself with her own loud snore. Her head darted up. She pushed her messy blonde hair out of her eyes to discover she was alone, lying on the floor of her bakery's kitchen. Daylight was beaming in through the glass fire exit door.

Groggy-headed and confused, she pushed herself to sitting, and glanced around to see piles upon piles of dirty dishes and bowls and utensils; washing up from the night before.

It all came back to her in a flood of emotion, and she leapt up to her feet.

It was the morning after the night of Randy Recommends! It was cupcake time!

Ali sprang to action, every limb and joint seeming to protest at her terrible sleeping position last night, as she whizzed from the storage fridge in the kitchen to the display fridge in the store, carrying armfuls of cupcakes with her on each trip. She could barely remember how exactly she'd come to fall asleep on her kitchen floor, beyond a vague recollection of thanking her friends for all their help in preparing the cupcakes and then sitting down to rest her aching legs, just for a moment. She'd evidently dozed off. That was to be expected, really, when you completed the marathon of all cupcake-making marathons.

Ali wished she had time to shower, but she didn't. All she could do was sweep her hair to the side and rebraid it more neatly. As she did, she spotted something she hadn't seen in all her rushing haste. There was a neat white cardboard box, just like the type she'd stockpiled to put takeout pastries in, sitting on the counter. It was wrapped in a large shimmering red bow.

Ali approached it curiously. Had Teddy left a gift behind for her? Or Delaney? It was the sort of sweet thing she could imagine one of them doing, but when they got the chance she had no idea.

Maybe it's from Nate! she thought excitedly, rushing to the counter. *A gesture of romantic intent!*

173

She fumbled with fatigued fingers to untie the bow and pull open the flaps of the box. Inside were six beautifully presented, scrumptious-looking cannoli. Handmade, by the looks of it.

There was a note attached. Curious, Ali unfolded it and read.

I trust you can keep our secret. Free pizza for life.

Ali folded Fat Tony's note away. It was a combination of a gift, a threat, and a thank-you. Ali wasn't quite sure what to make of it. She had no intention of cozying up to the local mobsters, though it would be a good idea to keep them as allies.

Too tempted not to, Ali quickly fished out a cannoli from the box and bit into its crisp shell. The creamy ricotta inside was sweet and delectable, and flavored with a hint of salted caramel. The sugar rush was just what Ali needed to help her overcome her grogginess from her poor night's sleep—or lack of sleep—on the kitchen floor.

Then she remembered where she was and what she needed to do. It was time to open the store and find out just how much influence Randy's radio show really had. Ali prayed it didn't all turn out to be a huge mistake on Delaney's part. It would be a very sore way to go, with a whole kitchen full of cupcakes...

Ali held her breath as she tiptoed inside the store. The doors and windows were covered by blinds, so there was no way of knowing yet if anyone had bothered to show up. As she crept toward the door, she felt like a kid on Christmas morning peering down the stairs to see how many presents there were under the tree. She was struck by a sudden strong memory of a gift she'd received one Christmas. A mini pink baking oven from her father.

She paused, remembering Teddy's words yesterday, about how her father would be crazy proud of her. Then she thought of her mother, and of how much she wanted to prove to her that her dreams weren't silly, that she could forge her own path in life.

She crept over to the window, almost too nervous to pull on the blind cord.

Yesterday you helped the mob and solved a murder, she told herself. *You can do this!*

In one flourishing gesture, she tugged on the blind cord and the blinds flew up.

Ali gasped. There was a crowd of people waiting outside her store. Old folks with their grandkids. Moms and dads with toddlers in tow. Couples standing hand in hand, and groups of teenagers in huddles.

Ali was astonished. They couldn't really all be here for her cupcakes, could they?

As she stared out the window, opened-mouthed, she spotted Marco and Emilio working the queue, handing out flyers and food samples for their rival pizzerias.

A giggle of excitement escaped Ali's throat. This was the exact way she'd dreamed it would be that first day when she'd stood here with Delaney, wearing the fake pearls Teddy had sent her in the mail.

As she twisted the lock, Ali glanced over at the pier. The Ferris wheel was turning at its tip, its lights flashing. She thought of her father.

She spotted a little silhouette on the railings. It was Django, the macaque, scurrying along, attempting to lure tourists into Lavinia Leigh's caravan.

A smile spread across Ali's lips. Lavinia had been right all along. Willow Bay was where she belonged. And she was going to make it.

She patted down her hair one last time and neatened her apron. Then she threw open the shop doors and the hungry hordes came flooding inside.

NOW AVAILABLE!

BEACHFRONT BAKERY: A MURDEROUS MACARON
(A Beachfront Bakery Cozy Mystery —Book 2)

"Very entertaining. I highly recommend this book to the permanent library of any reader that appreciates a very well written mystery, with some twists and an intelligent plot. You will not be disappointed. Excellent way to spend a cold weekend!"
--Books and Movie Reviews, Roberto Mattos (regarding Murder in the Manor)

BEACHFRONT BAKERY: A MURDEROUS MACARON is book #2 in a charming and hilarious new cozy mystery series by #1 bestselling author Fiona Grace, whose bestselling Murder in the Manor (A Lacey Doyle Cozy Mystery) has nearly 200 five star reviews.

Allison Sweet, 34, a sous chef in Los Angeles, has had it up to here with demeaning customers, her demanding boss, and her failed love life. After a shocking incident, she realizes the time has come to start life fresh and follow her lifelong dream of moving to a small town and opening a bakery of her own.

A rude tourist dies after eating his way up and down the boardwalk, and all eyes fall on Allison, as the police blame her new macarons. The macarons have a secret ingredient that is so delicious it has customers lining up and down the boardwalk—but they are not, she knows, the cause of death.

Allison, forced to clear her name and salvage her customers, has no choice but to retrace the victim's foodie trek up and down the boardwalk, and to figure out what he ate—or who he insulted—that could have gotten him killed.

With her beloved dog at her side, it is a race against time to crack the mystery and solve the crime before she loses her bakery—and her budding romance—for good.

A hilarious cozy mystery series, packed with twists, turns, romance, travel, food and unexpected adventure, the BEACHFRONT BAKERY series will keep you laughing and turning pages late into the night as you fall in love with an endearing new character who will capture your heart.

Books #3 (A PERILOUS CAKE POP), #4 (A DEADLY DANISH), #5 (A TREACHEROUS TART), and book #6 (A CALAMITOUS COOKIE) are also available!

Fiona Grace

Debut author Fiona Grace is author of the LACEY DOYLE COZY MYSTERY series, comprising nine books (and counting); of the TUSCAN VINEYARD COZY MYSTERY series, comprising five books (and counting); of the DUBIOUS WITCH COZY MYSTERY series, comprising three books (and counting); and of the BEACHFRONT BAKERY COZY MYSTERY series, comprising six books (and counting).

Fiona would love to hear from you, so please visit www.fionagraceauthor.com to receive free ebooks, hear the latest news, and stay in touch.

BOOKS BY FIONA GRACE

LACEY DOYLE COZY MYSTERY
MURDER IN THE MANOR (Book#1)
DEATH AND A DOG (Book #2)
CRIME IN THE CAFE (Book #3)
VEXED ON A VISIT (Book #4)
KILLED WITH A KISS (Book #5)
PERISHED BY A PAINTING (Book #6)
SILENCED BY A SPELL (Book #7)
FRAMED BY A FORGERY (Book #8)
CATASTROPHE IN A CLOISTER (Book #9)

TUSCAN VINEYARD COZY MYSTERY
AGED FOR MURDER (Book #1)
AGED FOR DEATH (Book #2)
AGED FOR MAYHEM (Book #3)
AGED FOR SEDUCTION (Book #4)
AGED FOR VENGEANCE (Book #5)
AGED FOR ACRIMONY (Book #6)

DUBIOUS WITCH COZY MYSTERY
SKEPTIC IN SALEM: AN EPISODE OF MURDER (Book #1)
SKEPTIC IN SALEM: AN EPISODE OF CRIME (Book #2)
SKEPTIC IN SALEM: AN EPISODE OF DEATH (Book #3)

BEACHFRONT BAKERY COZY MYSTERY
BEACHFRONT BAKERY: A KILLER CUPCAKE (Book #1)
BEACHFRONT BAKERY: A MURDEROUS MACARON (Book #2)
BEACHFRONT BAKERY: A PERILOUS CAKE POP (Book #3)
BEACHFRONT BAKERY: A DEADLY DANISH (Book #4)
BEACHFRONT BAKERY: A TREACHEROUS TART (Book #5)
BEACHFRONT BAKERY: A CALAMITOUS COOKIE (Book #6)